DAUGHTERS OF THE MOON

goddess
of the
night

LYNNE EWING

HBFC · NEW YORK

First edition
1 3 5 7 9 10 8 6 4 2
Printed in the United States of America

Library of Congress Cataloging-in-Publication Data

Ewing, Lynne.
Goddess of the night / Lynne Ewing.—1st ed.
p. cm.— (Daughters of the moon; #1)
Summary: Vanessa, who has always had the special power to become invisible,
discovers that she and her best friend Catty, a time-traveler, are goddesses of the moon
who must fight together to overcome the evil Atrox.
ISBN 0-7868-0653-2 (hard)
[1. Supernatural—Fiction. 2. Los Angeles (Calif.)—Fiction.] I. Title.

PZ7.E965 Go 2000
[Fic]—dc21   00-024210

Visit www.hyperionteens.com

*For Alessandra Balzer with deep gratitude.
This book would not have been possible without
her unlimited enthusiasm and encouragement.*

———∽∽∽———

*I would like to thank Marti Brooks,
Nadia Marquez, Andrew Mayesh, Nataly
Pena, Ivania Sandoval, and Mike Terrell for
sharing a small part of their lives with me.*

i

In ancient times, it was said that the goddess Selene drove the moon across the sky. Each night she followed her brother Helios, the sun, to catch his fiery rays and reflect the light back to earth. One night on her journey, she looked down and saw Endymion sleeping in the hills. She fell in love with the beautiful shepherd. Night after night she looked down on his gentle beauty and loved him more, until finally one evening she left the moon between the sun and the earth and went down to the grassy fields to lie beside him.

For three nights she stayed with him, and the moon, unable to catch the sun's rays, remained dark. People feared the dark moon. They said it brought death and freed evil forces to roam the black night. Zeus,

King of the Gods, was angered by the darkness and punished Selene by giving Endymion eternal sleep.

Selene returned to the moon and drove it across the night sky, but her love was too strong. She hid Endymion in a cave; and now, three nights each lunar month, she leaves the moon to visit her sleeping lover and cover him with silver kisses. In his sleep, Endymion dreams he holds the moon. He has given Selene many daughters to guard the night. They are powerful and beautiful like their mother, and mortal like their father.

CHAPTER ONE

VANESSA CLEVELAND cursed silently as she walked down the street. She couldn't shake the puzzling feeling that someone was following her. How could she forget it was the dark of the moon?

Overhead, low, thin clouds crept around the red-tile roofs and brought the ocean's cold. The cold didn't come to her all at once, but slowly and gently. She started to shiver and wasn't sure if it was from the cold or fear.

Vanessa had passed two houses when a soft scuttling sound made her stop and turn. The breeze picked up, and a bunch of dead leaves scraped down the sidewalk toward her. She felt a surge of relief and smiled. She tried to focus on something pleasant to keep her mind off her fear.

She thought of Michael Saratoga. His wild black hair hung in thick curls on his shoulders. He had strong, angular features, a sexy smile, and soft, dark eyes. She had liked him since the beginning of the school year when she first met him in Spanish class. But she had never imagined he would like her. Even now, fear of jinxing what might be forced her to push that sweet thought away. He made her feel all fire and ache down to her bones. That was good. That was also very bad. How could someone as different as she was ever expect to do a normal thing like have a boyfriend?

Abruptly she was aware that someone was on the street with her. She looked behind her. She expected to see a person in a bathrobe walking a dog, a wad of plastic sacks in hand, or a homeless person trudging down the middle of the road pushing a shopping cart.

But the street was empty. Was it the dark of the moon that was making her so jumpy?

She tried to concentrate on Michael again

and not think about the creeping shadows that seemed to be pressing closer with each step. Michael had asked her to dance eight times tonight at Planet Bang in Hollywood, and he would have spent more time with her if Morgan Page hadn't kept pulling him out onto the dance floor. Michael liked to dance, and Morgan danced better than she did.

She tried to remember the feel of Michael's cheek, his hand on her waist, his—

Something moved in the corner of her eye. She turned sharply. Whatever it was had slid across the shadows and then was gone.

She bent down and took off her heavy, wedge-soled shoes. The heels felt solid and lethal in her hands. She took two steps back and scanned the street. Then she knew. Relief broke through her fear. Her best friend, Catty, must be trailing her. Why hadn't she thought of that before? It wouldn't be the first time Catty had tried to scare her, thinking it was funny.

"Catty," she said. "I know it's you, come out." She spoke loudly, but a fine tremor had crept into her voice.

No one answered.

"Catty," she started again. Her voice was soft now, a whisper filled with fear.

She peered into the dark that clung to the side of a house. What had been there was gone. Had it only been an illusion of the dark?

Finally, she turned and started walking again, her bare feet steady on the cool cement. Her mother had warned her how dangerous it was for a girl to be out alone in Los Angeles at night. Now anger filled her and made a knot in her throat. It shouldn't be dangerous. Girls had a right to enjoy the night, to run wild under the moon and stars, not stay home huddled behind bolted doors.

Anger quickened her pace and made her brave. She gripped her shoes tightly. When she got to the corner, she stood defiantly under the steady glow of the street lamp. She waited a long time in the amber light. If it were someone with evil intent, a gangbanger, mugger, or desperate homeless person, they would have attacked by now.

She thought of Michael again, his hand on

her cheek. Had he been leaning down to kiss her when Morgan pulled him away?

Something skipped through the darkness. Something trying hard not to be seen. She was certain it was real this time, no trick of light and shadow. She turned to run and tripped over a tricycle lying on its side. Her shoes fell from her hands and scattered. The handlebar pushed painfully into her stomach.

The tricycle hadn't been there before. She would have seen something that size. Someone had crept behind her and placed it there. But how and when?

She left her shoes, pulled herself up, and ran. She didn't scream. A scream stole too much oxygen. She ran with savagery, her arms pumping at her sides. Already she could feel the arousal in her molecules, a soft and pleasant tremble. She could give in to her special power, but it was too chancy. She had a horrible feeling that what was happening to her now was somehow connected to her strange ability. She had always feared that one day someone would discover her secret.

If one person discovered the truth, she

would be hunted down, taken to some cheesy place like Las Vegas, and put on display. Then a new terror struck. Maybe the person skulking behind her was trying to frighten her into using her power. Perhaps a video recorder watched her, the owner hoping to capture the unthinkable on tape and sell it to the highest bidder.

Whoever it was was getting closer. Footfalls pounded softly in the grass behind her, gaining. She didn't glance back to see who it was.

Her molecules grew more excited, pinging to be free of gravity. She imagined herself, invisible, running through her clothes, her stalker stopping to pick up the organza peasant dress. Too risky.

Stay, she thought, stay. She had to concentrate to keep her molecules together. Her body longed to give in to the stretch of bone and muscle, and dissolve into a million fragments.

Then another sound made her heart wrench.

Other footsteps joined those of the person chasing her. More than one person this time, maybe more than two. Could it be even worse than she had first imagined?

What was her mother going to do when she found out her daughter was a freak? What would kids at school say? High school was hard enough without this, too. All she'd ever wanted was to be like everyone else.

She heard someone speaking. Then she realized the words were tumbling from her own lips in a high, keening pitch. What was she saying? Some forgotten prayer her mother had taught her when she was a child?

Her lips formed the strange words again. *"O Mater Luna, Regina nocis, adiuvo me nunc."*

Besides English, she knew only a little Spanish. These words were definitely not Spanish or English. Where had they come from?

From the corner of her eye, she saw a hand reach for her.

The words gathered on her lips again, hard and strong. She spit them out. *"O Mater Luna, Regina nocis, adiuvo me nunc."* The power of the words filled her as she spoke.

And then her chasers were gone. She kept running, afraid to trust what she knew was true. She was alone.

At the next block, she stopped and turned back. She rested her hands on her knees. Her breath came in gasps that stung her lungs. The street behind her was empty.

A trio of lawn flamingos stood in front of her. She stepped across the wet lawn and pulled on the serpentine neck of the first bird. The body tore free from the legs. She tossed the pink plastic bird aside and heaved the iron legs from the ground. The iron rods felt good in her hands.

She walked backward for half the block. She was only two blocks from Melrose Avenue now, and that meant people. She turned and ran toward the comforting traffic sounds, the garish neon lighting. The smells of Thai spices and northern Italian spaghetti sauces swirled deliciously around her as she barreled into the throng of kids crowding the sidewalk.

She stopped near a bus stop and stared back at the street from which she had fled. Four boys and a girl sat on the bus bench. The boys wore the uniform of modern primitives. Silver hoops pierced nipples, eyebrows, nose, and lips. Tattoos curled in languid lines around their necks and arms, and black leather vests flapped against their naked white chests like wicked pelts.

"Who you fighting?" the tall boy with the ratted black hair asked. He stared at her hand.

She glanced up. She held one flamingo leg like a javelin, aiming, her muscles taut, ready to strike.

She smiled to reassure the boy. He stepped back and stumbled off the curb. His eyes looked as if he saw something in Vanessa's face that frightened him.

"Go haunt another corner," the girl said.

Vanessa left them staring after her and started down Melrose. Her feet stepped in the black powdered grime that covered the street. She hated to think what foul things were gathering between her toes.

At home, the porch light blazed a welcome and covered the small craftsman-style house in a halo of gold light. The twisted olive tree stood rigid near the front walk. She crept to the side of the house and hid.

When she was sure no one had followed her, she walked to the back door, opened it, and stepped onto the back porch. She dropped the flamingo legs on the washing machine. The metal made a loud clank.

"Vanessa," her mother called.

She walked into the warm kitchen. The smells of coffee, glue, and pencil shavings wafted around her. A large bulletin board hung on the wall above the table. Her mother called it her inspiration board. A fanfare of sketches and bold-colored swatches were tacked to it now. She worked as a costume designer for the movies.

"You're late," her mother said and rushed to her. There was more fear in her eyes than anger. Her brown hair looked as if she had raked worried fingers through it. With cold hands she touched Vanessa's cheek, and then held her tightly. "I was worried about you. I hope you didn't walk home. You know how I feel about that."

"I got a ride," she lied. "Catty's mother picked us up."

Her mother shook her head. "Catty's mother wouldn't care if you stayed out all night." She didn't approve of the way Catty's mother let Catty run wild.

"I'm sorry I'm late," Vanessa said. She felt genuinely bad that she had caused her mother so much anxiety. "Planet Bang closed at *one* A.M., not midnight."

"On a school night? You know that's too late."

"I'll make sure I check the time next time."

"If there is a next time," her mother muttered.

"Mom, everyone goes to Planet Bang on Tuesday night. Tuesdays and Fridays are the only nights kids under twenty-one are allowed."

She stopped and followed her mother's stare. Her feet were black with city dirt, one big toe bleeding.

"For goodness sake, Vanessa, what did you do with your shoes?" her mother blurted out.

"The new shoes hurt my feet," Vanessa started another lie and stopped. Why did it seem like all conversations with her mother started or ended with lies? "I forgot them at Planet Bang. I'll call and see if someone found them."

"From now on I'm going to pick you up. This is not going to happen again. Ten-thirty is late enough for a school night. You should be in bed."

"All right." Vanessa stepped to the sink and poured herself a glass of water.

"Did anything happen tonight that you want to tell me about?" her mother said, suspicion rising in her voice.

"Nothing." Vanessa sipped the water. It tasted metallic and filled with chlorine. She spit it out.

"Something's wrong if you're drinking tap water," her mother said. "You'll poison yourself." She poured a glass of water from the cooler in the corner and handed it to Vanessa.

Vanessa swallowed the cool water, then stared at her mother. She had never thought of telling her mother the truth, but she had never felt so close to being exposed before this. What would her mother do? Maybe her mother had special powers of her own and had been waiting all this time for Vanessa to bring it up.

"Mom, are you . . ."

"What?"

"You know . . . different? I mean, besides the clothes." Her mother dressed on the cutting edge of fashion, wearing clothes before anyone even knew they were in style. That was her job. But sometimes it was embarrassing to have a mother so overly trendy. She had been wearing high-waters and pedal pushers two years ago, when everyone just thought her pants were too short.

"A psychic once told me I didn't march to the beat of a different drummer," her mother explained. "She said I had a whole band marching behind me."

"No, I mean really different." Vanessa's chin began to quiver. "Like in the freak category."

"Oh, honey." Her mother embraced her. "It's perfectly normal to feel like you don't fit in. It's part of growing up. You don't need to worry. Look at how popular you are at school. You get lots of telephone calls and invitations to parties."

If her mother only knew how much of her real self she had to keep hidden. Maybe kids at school liked her now, but what if they knew the truth?

"I have to do a lot to fit in, Mom." It wasn't self-pity. It was fact. "Kids aren't very accepting of someone who is really different."

"What's so different about you? You're pretty. You get good grades."

Did she dare tell her? Did she have a choice? If her life was in danger, maybe her mother could help. "Do you remember the night when I was a little girl and I woke up crying from a nightmare?"

"Which night? There were so many."

"The night you thought I was playing a game of hide-and-seek?"

"Yes—I found you sleeping in the bathroom and carried you back to bed."

"I wasn't hiding."

"What were you doing, then?"

"I was . . ." she stopped.

"Yes?"

She looked at her mother. How could she tell her that she had been invisible?

"I was . . . That was the night I found out . . ."

That had been the night she woke from a nightmare and couldn't see her body in the pale glow of the night-light. She had been terrified, and afraid to tell her mother. She had thought she had done something bad. Her mother had heard her crying and ran into her room. She had lifted her arms to be comforted, but her mother couldn't see her. That had frightened her even more. While her mother was searching the house for her, her molecules had come back together, but they had come back wrong. Her face had looked different. She had locked herself in the bathroom then, knowing her mother could never love her now. Sleep had finally taken her, and when she woke in the morning back in her own bed, she had looked normal.

"Vanessa, what did you find out that night?"

"Nothing. It's not important."

Her mother lifted her chin and looked into her eyes. "You're shaking."

"I just wish . . ."

"Tell me."

"I just wish I could be like everyone else."

"Is that all? Trust me, it's better to be an individual and to have your own idiosyncrasies." Her mother sat back at the table. "There's life after high school. Don't try too hard to blend in and be like everyone else. Kids who do lose something important." Her mother continued reciting what Vanessa called Standard Lecture No. 7.

She left her mother talking to the wall and went upstairs to the bathroom. She washed her feet. The water turned black and swirled down the drain.

Then she took a bath, put on pajamas, and went to her bedroom. She loved her room. She had window seats and shutters, flowered wallpaper, and a bed with too many pillows. Her mother called the decor "romance and drama," and said the room looked like it belonged to a fairy princess.

She turned on her computer and clicked on a program called Sky Show that she had purchased through *Astronomy* magazine. A thin slice of moon came on the screen. She looked at the date. According to the program, today should have been the first crescent moon, a time when she should have felt adventurous and filled with curiosity.

But the program had made an error. It was the dark of the moon tonight. Those three nights when the moon was completely dark and invisible from Earth had always had a strange hold on her. She felt nervous then, as if some part of her sensed danger. Catty's mother said superstitious people believed the dark moon brought death and destruction, and freed evil forces to roam the night.

A breeze ruffled the curtains. She hadn't left her window open. Maybe her mother had opened it. She shut the window and locked it, then sat on her bed and stared at her computer.

The door to her room opened. Her mother walked in.

"I came to kiss you good night," her mother said. "Why does it feel so cold in here?"

"My window was open. You didn't open it?"

"No, but that explains the draft I was feeling all night."

"My program's messed up. Did you play around with my computer?"

"Computer?"

"Right." Vanessa shook her head. "Silly idea."

Her mother kissed her quickly and started to leave.

"Mom?"

"Yes?"

"Do you know what this means?" She tried to repeat the sound of the words she had spoken earlier. *"Oh, Mah-tare Loon-ah, Re-gee-nah no-kis, Ad-you-wo may noonk."*

"That sounds like Latin." Her mother smiled. "That's what you did when you were a little girl."

"Speak Latin?"

"No," her mother said. "Hold your moon amulet that way."

She glanced down. After her father died, her nightmares had become stronger. Always the same dream—black shadows covering the full moon and then, like a specter, taking form and chasing her. She always woke clutching the silver moon amulet she wore around her neck. She was gripping it now.

"Good night, sweetheart." Her mother kissed the top of her head and left the room.

Vanessa stared at the night outside her window. Where would she have learned Latin? She knew it had to be connected to her power. If it weren't so late, she'd call Catty. Now she'd have to wait until tomorrow to find out if Catty had ever uttered words that she didn't understand.

She crawled under the covers. The cotton

sheets were sun-dried and ironed and filled with the smell of sunshine. She breathed in the fragrance and glanced back at her computer. For the first time she noticed her alarm clock with the luminous hands. It was turned toward the wall. She got up and turned it back to face her. Then she noticed her wristwatch. It was turned face-down. Odd. Maybe Catty had been playing around and left a calling card. She'd have a serious talk with her tomorrow and tell her that this time her jokes had gone too far.

CHAPTER TWO

CATTY AND VANESSA sat at the counter inside the Johnny Rockets diner. The smells of bacon and onions hung in the warm, thick air. Conversation whirled around them in a mad tangle of laughs and squeals, but only the thunder of motorcycles taking off outside was loud enough to drown the loud sing-songy music from the fifties and sixties.

"I swear I didn't go into your room last night." Catty's brown hair fell in perfect spirals around her face. When she tilted her head, the curls caught the sunlight pouring through the window.

"Someone turned my clock around," Vanessa said.

"Why would I turn your clock around?"

"Just to show me you had been there." Vanessa looked at her. "It wouldn't be the first time you had done something like that."

"But I was at Planet Bang with you." Catty had a slight smile that curled on her lips even when she frowned.

"I thought maybe you had tweaked time." She had hoped it had been Catty. "Who was in my room if it wasn't you?"

"Maybe no one," Catty pointed out. "Maybe you're creeping yourself out. You could have been nervous while getting ready. So you knocked over your clock and set it up facing the wall without noticing."

"Maybe," Vanessa agreed, but the nagging feeling that someone had been in her room wouldn't leave her.

"I can't believe you were so scared that you almost told your mother the truth about . . . you know." Catty flipped through the song titles in the Seeburg Wall-O-Matic. She picked up the nickels the waiter had left for the vintage machine, dropped two in the coin slot, and punched in a set of numbers. "Would you have told her about me, too?"

"No," Vanessa said. "Just me."

Charlie Brown boomed from the speakers, competing with the sizzle of hamburgers frying on the grill. A crowd of bikers walked in and straddled red seats at the counter.

"What would she have done?" Catty asked. "It's not something a mother expects to hear. 'Hey, Mom, did you know I can be as see-through as a ghost? Wanna see? I mean, not see.'" Catty laughed so hard the bikers turned and smiled at her.

Vanessa wiped the drop of chocolate running over the Johnny Rockets red emblem on the glass. "I'm not kidding, Catty, it wasn't just the dark of the moon. Someone was following me."

"I know one way we can check it out." Catty dug her spoon into the whipped cream on top of the shake.

"No," Vanessa said firmly. "I told you. Never

again. Not after last time." The truth was, Vanessa found Catty's power frightening.

"You always say that, and then you end up changing your mind."

"I guess. Want my tomatoes?"

"Last night made you all messed up." Catty took the tomatoes and tucked them into her burger.

Vanessa didn't want to talk about last night anymore. It was better forgotten, like a nightmare. "I looked for you at school today."

"I was hopping time," Catty said. She picked up a French fry covered with chili and cheese and pushed it into her mouth.

"You got to stop doing that! You're missing too many tests."

"My mother doesn't care."

"But you should." Sometimes Vanessa felt jealous of Catty's relationship with her mother. Catty's mother didn't care if she missed school, because she knew Catty was different. She also wasn't Catty's biological mother. She had found Catty walking along the side of the road in the desert between Gila Bend and Yuma when Catty was six years old. She'd planned to turn her over to the authorities in Yuma, but when she saw Catty make time change, she decided Catty was an extraterrestrial, separated from her parents, like E.T., and that it was her duty to protect her from government officials who would probably dissect her. She brought Catty to Los Angeles, knowing that in a city where anything goes, a child from another planet could fit in.

Catty had only two memories of the time before she was six. One of a crash, the other of a fire. Both were only flashes of memory and didn't reveal much about her past. When her power was strong enough, Catty planned to go back to the time before she was six.

Vanessa rolled down the paper wrapper that swaddled the hamburger. She opened her mouth wide and bit down. Mayonnaise, pickle juice, and mustard ran down her chin.

The waiter came back. "How's the hamburger?" he asked.

"Great," Catty said and let a piece of tomato fall from her mouth.

The waiter laughed and picked up the tomato from the counter, then walked away.

"You are so gross!"

Catty punched her playfully. "Vanessa, I'm just trying to get your mind off last night. You probably had some dog running after you, or a homeless person who likes to play games. Let's go back and see."

"No."

"Why not?" Catty persisted, sipping her shake.

"You know why. I'm too afraid we'll go back some time and get stuck."

"So what? All you'd have to do is relive the time. It would be fun. We'd know what was going to happen."

"You don't know if that's how it really works."

"That's because I've never gotten stuck," Catty pointed out.

When Catty had first tried time traveling, it had only been in short bursts. Then she had learned that if she concentrated she could make hops in time up to twenty-four hours into the past or the future. Catty figured if she lost her power and couldn't return to the present, she would just relive a day or, if she had jumped time into the future, lose a day. Vanessa wasn't so sure. There was also the tunnel, the hole in time they had to go through. She was terrified of getting stuck there.

"I don't know why you worry so much," Catty said, taking another bite.

"Forget it. It was probably a homeless person, like you said," Vanessa insisted. "I don't need to see."

Catty spoke with her mouth full. "We should check it out. To be sure."

Vanessa plucked a French fry from the globs of melted cheese and chili. She twirled it in the raw onions and slipped it into her mouth.

"You remember the first time you took me traveling?" Vanessa said with a smile.

"Yeah," Catty giggled. "You about broke my eardrums in the tunnel."

They had been watching TV after Catty's ninth birthday party, waiting for Vanessa's mother to pick her up. Catty wanted to show her something special. Vanessa had thought it was another birthday present. Instead, Catty had

grabbed her hand, and a strange heaviness crack-
led through the air. The fine hairs on her arm
stood on end before the living room had flashed
away with a burst of white light. Suddenly, they
were whirling downward through a dark tunnel.
The air inside felt thick enough to hold. She
could barely breathe. Her screams bounced back
at her until the sound became deafening. Just
when it had grown unbearable, they fell with a
hard crash back into the living room. Only, the
living room was different now. Sunlight came
through the windows. Wrapping paper and rib-
bons were scattered over the gray-green rug. Then
they had peeked into the dining room, and
Vanessa had seen herself, sitting at the table eating cake and ice cream. She had been too shocked
to scream again. Catty stole into the kitchen, and
returned with two pieces of cake, and before
Vanessa could ask her what was going on, they
were back in the hated tunnel with its thick, sucking air and bad smells. Instead of landing in the
living room, they had landed five blocks away on
someone's front porch.

"I got in so much trouble." Vanessa shook

her head. "My mother thought I had wandered off." She couldn't tell her mother what had really happened. Her mother would never have believed her, anyway.

"But the cake was worth it," Catty said.

"You ate my slice." Vanessa smiled. "I was crying because the tunnel scared me so much. Remember?"

"It's not like you didn't get even."

"You deserved it," Vanessa teased. "You were always getting me in trouble." Vanessa had planned for weeks, practicing with her teddy bear until she could make it invisible with her. Then one Sunday while they were playing in Catty's backyard, she had hugged Catty and scrunched her eyes in concentration until she felt her molecules pinging. She had opened her eyes. Catty was becoming a dusty cloud. The cloud swirled around, and Vanessa had seen a look of utter astonishment on Catty's face before she became completely invisible. Success! Her plan had worked. Vanessa's molecules had exploded outward in complete delight. At first Catty had buzzed around the backyard like a balloon losing its air. Vanessa couldn't see her, but she could feel her air currents. But then she had started to get cold and wanted to become visible again. Vanessa wasn't as practiced as Catty. An hour later, even with total concentration, she had only managed to make parts of them visible. When Catty saw her hand floating, unattached to her arm, she had started crying. That had made Vanessa more nervous. It had taken her hours to get them back together, whole and right.

Catty nudged her. "You should use your gift more often. Practice makes perfect and all that."

But Vanessa had felt so bad about what she had done to Catty that she had sworn never to use her power again. Since then she had tried to control her molecules, but in times of intense emotion, her molecules had more power than her ability to restrain them and the light from a full moon seemed to fuel their change.

"Hurry up and eat," Catty prodded her.

"Why? We've got plenty of time."

Two minutes later, Catty put her hand on Vanessa's shoulder. Her eyes were dilated as though a powerful energy were building in her brain. Vanessa glanced at Catty's watch. The minute hand started moving backward.

"Don't," she begged. "This will be the third time we've left without paying."

"But they won't know. As far as they'll know, we never came in. It will be last night for them."

"But we've still eaten their food without paying for it."

Catty rolled her eyes. "The food didn't *exist* yesterday, so why does it matter?"

"It just feels wrong, and I told you I didn't want to go back, anyway."

The hands on Catty's watch stopped moving.

"You need to go back and see that nothing was there, or you'll never stop thinking about last night."

"I won't," Vanessa said. "Besides, Morgan just walked in."

"So?"

"She's been around too many times when we've switched time. I think she suspects something."

"Morgan doesn't suspect anything. She can't."

"I know she can't, but she's been asking

questions," Vanessa said. Catty was sure that when she went back in time, people had no sensation of returning to the past. But Vanessa thought people sensed the changes in the length of an hour, the confusion of memory, and a rash of déjà vu.

"Besides," Vanessa added. "I told her we'd go over to the Skinmarket with her."

"Why do you want to hang out with her when she tried to take Michael away from you?"

"She didn't try to take Michael away. She's a better dancer than I am, and Michael likes to dance."

"I don't want to hang out with her," Catty complained. "She makes me feel like I'm not clean enough."

"That's just your imagination."

Vanessa reached for her soda. As she put her hand out, Catty clasped her wrist. The hands of the watch started spinning backward.

"No!" Vanessa screamed as "Love Potion Number 9" began playing on the Seeburg.

The bikers turned and stared at her. Morgan waved, and her lustrous hair swung out as the air pressure changed.

Vanessa dropped the hamburger and clutched the strap of her messenger bag. Her skin prickled with static electricity. A white flash burned reality away, and the diner roared from them with the speed of light.

That was the last thing Vanessa remembered as she fell into the tunnel with Catty. She kept her eyes closed as they spun downward, and her stomach lurched. She hated the smell and feel of the air. Without looking, she knew Catty was watching the backward-spinning hands on her glow-in-the-dark wristwatch. When they arrived at their time destination, she'd put all her concentration into stopping the flow of time, and they'd fall back into time and reality.

They landed on a lawn with a heavy thud.

She looked up. The smells of onions and frying hamburgers still wafted in the air around them, but it was dark now, and they were on the street where she had walked the night before.

"You've got to work on the landings," Vanessa groaned and pulled herself up.

"I told you, a fall is the only way out."

Vanessa looked around. The night was silent

except for the occasional scrape of palm fronds overhead. Then, in the distance, she heard soft, running footsteps and the rapid, pounding steps of the person who had chased her.

"Let's go see who it was," Vanessa said. "I mean, who it *is*."

"Right," Catty agreed.

They bolted and ran wildly down the street. The cool evening breeze stung their faces. Their footsteps pounded softly on the dew-wet pavement. Vanessa knew at once that the second set of footfalls she had heard the night before were those that she and Catty were making now.

A block ahead, she could see herself, barefoot and running rapidly. Someone was chasing her. It was impossible at this distance to identify her pursuer, who was dressed in black and wearing a cap.

She heard herself shout the strange prayer in the language she didn't understand.

At the same time her pursuer glanced back. The person must have seen them, but Vanessa couldn't be sure. Suddenly, the person darted across a lawn and into the shadows.

"This way," Catty said.

Vanessa followed her to a shortcut between two houses and into a narrow alleyway. She whispered, "Do you think whoever it is saw two of me?"

"If so, they'll never chase you again."

Vanessa almost laughed, but she was too breathless and excited with anticipation to see who it was.

They ran down the alleyway to the next block, then crossed another street.

"Whoever's following you should be around here someplace," Catty whispered.

They crouched low and stepped cautiously down the alley.

Without streetlights, the backyards were darker, the shadows deeper. Vanessa peered over the fence. She didn't see anyone, but she heard the soft, padding steps of someone trying hard to be quiet.

They ducked and hurried along a length of fence to a garage. She looked around the corner of the garage. A shadowy figure ran across the back lawn to the next house.

She motioned to Catty, and they stepped silently forward. When they got to the next house, they gazed over a row of garbage cans into the tomblike quiet in the yard beyond. If her pursuer had been there, the person must have heard their movements and hidden.

Catty nudged her and pointed.

A thicker shadow formed between the house and a twisting cypress. It looked like someone was standing there. Vanessa was sure the person was looking directly at her even though she couldn't see the eyes. And then the shadow whispered, *I'll find you later when you're alone.* She wasn't sure she'd heard it, as much as felt it like a soft rustling across her mind.

Panic seized her.

"Did you hear that?" Vanessa asked.

"What?"

"Take us back, Catty. Now!"

CHAPTER THREE

VANESSA FELT HERSELF jerked away. Her neck whipped backward, and then the night zipped away with a sudden flash and roar. Vanessa clutched Catty's hand as they spiraled through the tunnel. Her stomach wobbled with nausea, and she knew if they didn't stop soon she was going to lose her hamburger.

They landed with a hard knock. The air left her body. Pain spun thin and sharp inside her skull. She closed her eyes against the harsh fluorescent lighting.

A buzzing sound filled her ears. She soon realized it was laughter.

"Dang! Girls," someone shouted and the laughter grew. She struggled to open her eyes.

She was vaguely aware that Catty was squealing and calling her name.

"Catty," she whispered. This time Catty's voice penetrated her aching head.

"Vanessa, we're in the boy's locker room and the water polo team just finished practice."

Water polo? She was still in a dreamlike trance. Michael was on the water polo team. She'd get to see him. That made her smile. "Michael."

New laughter echoed off the walls. "She wants to see you, Michael."

Her nose touched something wet. She looked down. A wet blue Speedo lay in the chlorine-smelling water near her face. Her head shot up. The boy's locker room!

As quickly as she had looked up, she looked down again. A scream caught in her throat.

"Catty!" she yelled. Keeping her head down, she stood. She was never going to forgive Catty for this landing,

"Here." Catty was giggling in pure delight.

Vanessa found Catty, yanked her hard, and

pulled her through the throng of naked boys.

"Did you get to see what you came looking for?" someone said.

Embarrassment made her molecules disarrange. "Not now," she whispered.

A shrill whistle made the laughter stop. Vanessa spread her fingers. Coach Dambrowsky plodded into the locker room, his tennis shoes squishing water. His forehead and nose were sunburned.

Vanessa ducked around him, her hands in front of her face. He must have sidestepped because she ran into his soft stomach.

"Excuse me." She tried to worm past him.

"Wait a minute!" He grabbed at her arm. His fingers whipped through her disorganized molecules. "What the—?"

This time he caught Catty.

"You two are busted," he said and brushed flecks of dandruff from his blue sweatshirt.

Catcalls filled the locker room.

"You girls should be ashamed of yourselves. Don't you have any modesty?" Coach Dambrowsky scolded.

"If we were boys in a girls' locker room you'd

snicker and pat us on the back," Vanessa argued from behind her hands. She spread her fingers to see how angry he looked. The sunburn had turned crimson. He was pissed.

"Let's see, who do we have here?" Coach licked his thumb and pulled pink demerit slips from his pocket. "Let me see your face."

Vanessa slowly brought her hands down.

Coach looked surprised. Was her face disarranged?

She glanced at Catty. She could tell by Catty's expression that she looked fine. She took a deep breath. How was she going to explain this to her mother?

"Vanessa Cleveland. Of all the girls in the sophomore class, I expected more from you."

He looked at Catty with a dour face. "And Catty Turner." He didn't seem surprised that Catty was there. He handed a slip to each of them. "Demerit slips, girls."

"It's a nice color of pink." Catty smirked.

"Yes, sir," Vanessa mumbled. Head down, she ran back, picked up her messenger bag from a puddle of water, and hurried outside.

Catty waited for her at the door.

"I can't believe you brought us back here," Vanessa said. "What's everyone going to say? They'll think we snuck in there."

"So what?" Catty wadded her demerit slip and tossed it away. "It's not like I did it on purpose."

"Catty, you'll just be in more trouble," Vanessa said. "You can't throw away your demerit slips."

"We wouldn't have demerit slips if you'd let me tweak time a little. Want to?"

"You can't always use your power to get us out of trouble. You rely too much on changing time to duck responsibility."

"Who made you my mother?"

"Sorry." Vanessa adjusted the bag on her shoulder. "But it's dangerous."

"Dangerous?" Catty acted as if they'd never had this conversation before.

"What if you get stuck in the tunnel?"

"If something went wrong I'd just fall out. It's not real. It just feels like I'm going faster than the speed of light."

"Maybe." Vanessa leaned against the sun-soaked wall. It was as hot as a fire brick and felt good against her throbbing head. She wasn't as convinced as Catty. The tunnel felt like a real place to her. The times she had ventured a peek, it seemed to stretch to infinity. "Did you ever think that maybe that's the world we belong in? That somehow we got stuck in some kind of time warp? Maybe that's why your mother found you walking along the side of the road."

"That would explain me, but what about you?" Catty stood next to her. They had tried many theories to explain their powers. The time warp was just another one.

"I'm afraid you could get stuck in that world."

"That's crazy," Catty said. "Won't happen."

"Just promise to be careful, or I'll get mushy on you and tell you how much you mean to me."

Catty punched her gently. "Stop. I've got it under control. Loosen up, all right?"

Vanessa looked at Catty. She felt something dreadful gnawing at her.

"So who do you think was following me?" Vanessa pulled her sunglasses from her pocket.

The fall had cracked the lens. She tossed them into her bag.

"I think you've got a mystery man. Someone with a crush on you."

"A secret admirer?" Vanessa joked.

"Half the boys at school have crushes on you."

As if to prove her point, two seniors walked by, swinging skateboards.

"Hey, Vanessa," one said.

"Looking good," the other added.

"Hi," Vanessa waved.

"See," Catty pointed out.

"I'm just friendly." Vanessa shrugged, and then she remembered what had really bothered her about the night. "Did you hear anything?"

"No. What did you think you heard anyway?"

"I thought someone said, 'I'll find you later when you're alone.'"

"I didn't hear that," Catty mused. "But if I had, I would have been freaked!"

Vanessa lifted her face, and with the late afternoon sun beating down on her, it was impossible to remember how dead scared she had felt the night before. The terror had slipped away in a drowsy way, like smoke after a fire.

"A mystery man," Vanessa repeated softly.

"Definitely," Catty said. "At first he was probably too shy to approach you, some loner walking home from Planet Bang, then he gets up his nerve to talk to Vanessa Cleveland, the most popular girl at La Brea High—"

"I am not."

"Be quiet, it's my story. He goes to talk to you and you panic and run away. Now he's got to chase you down to tell you he's sorry he scared you. Then he turns and sees us, and now he's really embarrassed so he hides. I wonder who it is?"

"Someone like Michael Saratoga," Vanessa whispered as last night slipped deeper into memory. "I hope it's Michael."

"You talking about me?" a voice said.

Her eyes flew open.

Michael walked over to her. He wore a short-sleeved T-shirt. Barbed-wire tattoos circled his tan arms. He had just come from the boy's locker room and his hair was still wet. His dark round eyes made her think of an ancient sun god trapped in L.A.'s urban nightmare. She liked the way his eyes looked at her. His lips curled around perfect white teeth. She wanted those lips to want her. Her molecules hummed. Could he hear her desire like a soft growl rushing through her spreading molecules? Damn invisibility. Maybe if she thought of the upcoming geography test, her molecules would stay.

"Hi, Michael." She tried to keep the excitement out of her voice.

He stepped closer, and a whiff of spicy deodorant and chlorine enveloped her. She breathed deeply.

He sniffed. "You smell like onions."

She smelled her hands. The aroma of the onions from the Johnny Rockets chili fries clung to the tips of her fingers. "Sorry." What magic did those dark eyes have to make her apologize?

"I like onions."

"Me, too," she said. "I didn't see you after school."

"I had water polo practice." Michael smiled. "I guess you saw me there."

She felt the blush rise to her cheeks, and then

thought, so what? He should be the one blushing. She smiled with an insolence her mother would have scolded her for. She knew he was blushing behind his dark cheeks by the way he shifted his feet and cleared his throat.

"You want to hang out on Saturday?" he asked.

"What do you have planned?" Was this a date? She stomped her foot, trying to make her molecules obey. Don't go invisible now.

"Something special." The tips of his fingers brushed across the fine hairs of her arm. Her stomach fluttered and her molecules tingled with delight.

"Sure."

"See you Saturday, then," he said. "I'll pick you up at seven." She watched him walk away, his backpack bouncing against his shoulder.

CHAPTER FOUR

VANESSA AND CATTY walked across the school lawn. New worry started buffeting her happiness.

"What will I do if Michael tries to kiss me?"

"I don't know, open your mouth a little, I guess."

"I'm serious," Vanessa scolded. "What am I going to do? Just looking at him makes my molecules vibrate. The last time I tried to have a boyfriend, I couldn't control it. I never even got one kiss."

"Let your molecules sing," Catty said. "Maybe he'll like it. Besides you don't know it will happen this time. Have you been practicing with your power like I told you?"

One look and Catty knew she hadn't. "When you're alone you need to make yourself invisible," Catty explained. "Visible, invisible. Just like exercises. How else are you going to learn how to control it? You should practice every day."

"That won't help me now. What if my molecules go off on their own?" Vanessa wondered. "What if I scare him? Maybe he'll think I'm a ghost or something evil."

"You should appreciate your gift more. I mean, just think what you could do with it. I know what I'd do."

"What?"

"I'd spy on people and copy answers to all the tests. You waste it."

"All my problems seem to come from what you call a 'gift.' I wish we could be like everyone else."

"Speak for yourself. I like what I can do," Catty said. "You want a Coke?"

The fact that they were freaks never bothered Catty as much as it bothered Vanessa. Maybe it was because Catty's mother encouraged her to use her power.

"No, thanks." Vanessa sat on a cement bench facing a bank of outside lockers. "I'll wait for you here."

She looked down at the amulet that hung around her neck. She seldom took it off, but she unclasped it now and studied the face of the moon etched in the metal. Sparkling in the sunlight, it wasn't pure silver but reflected pinks and blues and greens. Maybe who she was had something to do with this moon charm that was given to her at birth. Catty had one, too. That's how they had first noticed each other at the park in third grade. They had been playing soccer on opposing teams, chasing the ball down the field. When they saw the silver moon dangling from each other's neck, they'd stopped running and let the ball go out of bounds.

"Where'd you get that?" Catty had asked, ignoring her jeering teammates.

"I got it as a gift the night I was born," Vanessa said. "Where'd you get yours?"

"Don't know. I've always had it. I never take it off."

"Me, neither," Vanessa said.

The referee blew her whistle and the game continued, but Vanessa couldn't focus on the ball. She kept turning to look at Catty. Twice she kicked the ball out of bounds, and once she collided with one of her own teammates.

Afterward the two teams went out for pizza. She and Catty shared a double-cheese pepperoni with pineapple and anchovies. They had been best friends ever since. It had taken longer for them to share their unique talents. What Catty called their gifts.

Maybe it wasn't a gift, but a curse, and if she got rid of the charm, her strange ability to become invisible would also go away. But she felt too uncomfortable when she took it off. She wondered why that was.

CHAPTER FIVE

CATTY CAME BACK with a Coke and sat next to Vanessa.

Morgan Page ran up to them. She dropped her purse and swirled. "What do you think?" She wore a bare, breezy sundress. It was too skimpy for the school dress code, so she wore sleeves over the halter sundress during classes. Now she shed the sleeves and showed off her solar-glow tan, the best in the school. Expensive salon highlights added luster to her already perfect hair. She picked up her purse and pushed her yellow shades into her hair.

"Where have you been? I walked all the way to Johnny Rockets looking for you. I must be glistening with sweat."

Catty leaned into Vanessa muttering, "She's got to be the only person in the world who thinks her sweat is pretty."

Morgan didn't hear Catty over her own running talk. "I swear I saw you two sitting at the counter. I thought we were supposed to meet at Johnny Rockets."

Vanessa gave Catty a quick, angry look.

Morgan watched them with curiosity.

"You couldn't have seen us," Catty said. "We were in the boys' locker room."

She elbowed Vanessa. Vanessa held up her demerit slip as proof.

Morgan couldn't be lured away from her questioning. "I could have sworn I saw you two munching on burgers, and then you were gone."

"We weren't there," Vanessa insisted.

Morgan stopped. She eyed the silver moon charm in Vanessa's hand.

"That would go perfectly with my dress." She reached for it.

Vanessa quickly clasped the necklace around her neck.

"You always wear it," Morgan said. "Don't you ever get tired of it?"

"Sometimes, I guess," Vanessa lied, and wished she hadn't. She didn't want Morgan to think the amulet was something she would ever lend out.

"I saw you talking to my hottie."

"Who?" Vanessa asked.

"Michael, of course. Was he asking about me?"

"Michael asked Vanessa to go out with him," Catty informed her smugly.

Morgan seemed upset, but only for a moment. She smiled and pulled the yellow shades back on her perfect nose. "So you're going out with Michael."

"Yes." Vanessa felt a little embarrassed.

"Be careful."

"Be careful of what?"

"You know, he conquers the land and leaves it desolate."

"Translation?" Catty's eyebrows raised.

"He makes like he's all vulnerable and sensitive so you start trusting him and then he takes advantage," Morgan responded knowingly.

"How can he take advantage if you don't let him?" Catty demanded.

"Guys have their way. Sometimes they think it's their due."

"Michael doesn't seem—"

"That's my point exactly," Morgan continued. "That's how he gets away with it. And I bet you haven't even kissed."

"So what?" Catty was exasperated.

"You'll see," Morgan warned.

"I didn't know you liked him," Vanessa said.

"Please," Morgan snorted. "I call every good-looking guy my hottie. He's nothing special."

Vanessa sensed that Morgan was upset, maybe even jealous, but before she could say more, Morgan's radar picked up someone else.

"There's Serena," Morgan said. "She's such a freaky dresser."

Serena Killingsworth walked toward them, carrying her cello in a brown case. Her short hair, currently colored Crayola-red, was twisted into bobby-pin curls. A nose ring glistened on the side of her nose. She wore purple lipstick, red-brown shadow around her green eyes, and a smile that seemed to hold a secret. She was new at school. Vanessa liked her look and especially admired the way she seemed so oblivious to what other people thought about her.

"Hey, Morgan." Serena set down the cello. Her chartreuse fingernails worked the combination on her locker.

"She's such a walking rummage sale," Morgan whispered disapprovingly.

"I like it," Vanessa said.

"I like it, too," Catty agreed.

Morgan sighed. "Okay, she has her moments. But she's got a bad addiction to the bizarre."

"How could you know that? She's only been in school a few weeks," Vanessa argued. "I heard her family moved here from Long Beach so she could take classes at UCLA along with her high school classes."

"Having brains doesn't mean you're not weird," Morgan said, casting a sly glance at Catty. "Her best friend is on probation, some gang girl from East L.A."

"That doesn't mean anything." Irritation buzzed inside Vanessa.

"I hear they stay out all night. I bet they're into some kinky stuff."

Serena opened her locker and cast an amused look at Morgan.

Morgan pulled peach hand lotion from her purse and spread it over her arms. "Too bad her brother's such a surf nazi. What a loss. He's the kind of guy you'd like to spend the night with. But the only thing he's looking for are waves. What is it with this town, anyway? Do all the gorgeous guys just wake up one morning and decide they're too good for women?"

"Don't you think there are other things to worry about?" Catty was losing her patience.

Vanessa gave her a quick look. She wasn't in the mood to referee another fight between Catty and Morgan.

Morgan didn't seem to hear her. "Collin is as cute as Michael," she continued. "Almost. I don't know how he got such a freaky sister. Hey, why don't you ask Serena about Michael if you don't believe me?"

"Has she dated him?" Vanessa asked.

Morgan laughed dismissively. "I can't believe you don't know."

"What?" Catty and Vanessa said together.

Morgan leaned in closer. "She's a fortune-teller. She can answer your questions about guys. She charges twenty dollars a pop. But I swear it's worth fifty."

"How did you find out so much so quickly?" Catty was amazed.

"I ask." Morgan nodded wisely. "She's read my fortune twice already."

"She probably just tells you what you want to hear," Vanessa scoffed.

Morgan shook her head. "It's spooky. I swear. With her tarot cards, it's like she knows things no one can know. Don't ask her anything you're afraid to find out because you might not like the answer. And you have to go alone. That's her only rule. You need to go see her, Vanessa."

"Why?"

"She'll tell you just how bad your broken heart will be; some girls never recover from Michael Saratoga."

Vanessa didn't think that sounded like

Michael. He was polite and sweet, and she liked his gentle humor. He never told raunchy jokes, or made vulgar comments like so many of the guys at school did.

Serena picked up her cello and walked over to them. "Were you one of those girls, Morgan?"

"What girls?"

"You know, one of the girls who never recovered from a broken heart?" There was a sparkle in Serena's green eyes.

"Damn." Morgan's eyes narrowed. "See what I mean?"

"How did you know what we were talking about?" Vanessa asked.

"I have acute hearing," Serena said.

Morgan gave her a dirty look.

Serena stuck out her pierced tongue, showing off the stainless-steel barbell.

"Cool." Catty had already pierced her belly button. Vanessa wanted to but hadn't had gotten up the nerve yet.

Morgan wrinkled her nose in disgust. "Germ central." She walked away, but she kept casting backward glances as if she were afraid Serena was going to put a curse on her.

"Here." Serena handed Vanessa and Catty each a piece of paper. "My home address. Come by any time you want your fortune read. And come alone." She picked up her cello and started toward the bus stop. "Catch you later."

Catty tossed her paper on the ground. "Too endlessly weird. On a scale of one to infinity, she gets infinity plus a billion. I don't believe anyone can see into the future."

"That sounds strange coming from you." Vanessa glanced at her watch. "We're supposed to meet my mother, and with your insane time travel we're going to be late."

"I'll just take us back an hour," Catty started.

"No." Vanessa stopped her. "We're going to do it the old-fashioned way. We're going to walk and I'm going to get yelled at for being late."

Vanessa stared at the paper Serena had given her as she and Catty walked up La Brea Avenue toward Melrose. Was what Morgan had said about Michael true? She tucked the paper in her pocket.

CHAPTER SIX

FRIDAY AFTERNOON, campus security roamed the hallways and parking lot at La Brea High School, trying to stop surfers, skaters, gangsters, and ravers from cutting the rest of the school day and starting an early weekend.

"Come on," Catty called. "They'll never catch us if we sneak off campus through the back field. I've done it a million times."

Vanessa hesitated. "But we'll get suspended if they catch us."

Catty giggled and pulled Vanessa forward. "Whoever thought of suspending students for cutting classes? It's exactly what they wanted in the first place."

"It goes on your permanent record."

"Don't you want to ask my mother if she knows what those words mean, the ones you said the other night?" Catty smiled persuasively.

"I can wait till after school."

"I told you she's busy tonight. Now's your only chance."

"All right." Vanessa sighed.

"Great," Catty said. "Let's hurry."

They ran down the narrow weed-filled corridor between the gym and music building. Grasshoppers and moths scattered in front of their feet. A trill of flutes and the honk of a tuba came from inside the music room.

At the end of the buildings, they stopped and scanned the football field. It was empty.

"Walk slowly," Catty warned. "If security calls us, just turn back and pretend we didn't hear the bell. Or . . ."

"Or?" Vanessa said.

"Or just make us invisible."

"Right," Vanessa mumbled sarcastically, and glanced behind them. Her heart thumped against her chest. Catty was always talking her into doing things she knew were wrong, like staying out late, cutting classes, and making prank calls.

They squeezed under the wire mesh fence and hurried down a side street to La Brea.

"There, see? Not so hard." Catty grinned as they headed down La Brea Avenue toward Third.

The Darma Bookstore was between Polka Dots and Moonbeams Dress Shop and Who's on Third? café. Brass bells on long leather cords tingled in harmony when they pushed through the door. Smoky incense curled sinuously around them and filled the air with a pungent scent.

"Hi, Mom," Catty called.

The store always gave Vanessa a feeling of peace and security. Water bubbled from fountains set in stone planters near the door and the chanting of Tibetan monks flowed from speakers set in the wall. Books, packages of candles, incense, prayer beads, crystals, and essence oils lined white shelves in neat arrays.

Catty's mother, Kendra, pushed through the blue curtains separating the back room from the store.

"You got out of school early," she said with a smile and winked. She was tall and bony, with a narrow face and long brown hair streaked with gray. She wore a stunning purple dress that flowed around her when she walked. The sleeves were long and touched the tips of her fingers. A pair of red-framed reading glasses dangled on a chain around her neck and clicked against the rose crystals she wore. She believed in the healing energy stored in crystals. Today she also wore the pouch given to her by a traditional doctor on one of her trips to Botswana.

She hugged Catty, and then put both hands around Vanessa's face and kissed her. She smelled of sesame oil, camphor, cardamom, and cinnamon. She rubbed the spicy concoction into her temples several times during the day to stimulate her senses.

She looked at Vanessa a long time. Vanessa always had the feeling that Catty's mother was trying to detect something different about her.

"I was just making ginger tea. Let's go in the back. It'll help detoxify your body and digestive system."

Catty rolled her eyes. "Mom, don't you have anything that regular people like?"

"I just grated the ginger and the milk is warm," Kendra went on as if she hadn't heard Catty's complaint. "You'll love it."

They followed her through the bookcases to a small kitchen in the back of the store and sat down at the oak table. Pictures of UFO sightings and a huge poster of deep space taken from the Hubble telescope hung on the walls.

"Did you girls have a good day at school?" Kendra asked, and started to pour them each a cup of milky ginger tea.

Catty put her hand over the top of the cup. "Don't you have any cocoa mix?"

"The ginger tea is better for you."

Catty rolled her eyes.

Vanessa smiled. She liked Catty's mom.

Kendra sighed. "All right." Then she looked at Vanessa. "I suppose you want hot chocolate, too?"

"Yes, please." Vanessa studied the picture of a fuzzy flying saucer hovering over the desert in Arizona.

Kendra reheated the milk in the microwave, then spooned cocoa into two mugs. She poured milk over the cocoa and brought the mugs back to the table and sat down.

Vanessa opened her messenger bag and pulled out a piece of paper on which she had carefully written the words she had spoken on the night she was being chased. She handed the paper to Kendra. "I was wondering if you knew what this meant."

Kendra put on her reading glasses. Her lips moved as she read the words to herself.

"These words just came to you?"

Vanessa nodded.

Kendra examined the words closely. "The words are misspelled, but even so, I know it's Latin. It appears you were praying to the moon to protect you." She smoothed the paper and ran her index finger under the words as she read, "O Mother Moon, Queen of the night, help me now."

Vanessa put down her cocoa, unable to speak. She lifted her moon amulet with trembling fingers and stared at it.

"Mother Moon," she repeated, then she

looked at Catty and saw she was reacting the same way.

"Freaky," Catty said.

"Oh, it's not so strange." Nothing ever seemed to surprise Kendra. "You and Catty have always had a connection to the moon. I suppose you could have seen this prayer in a book a long time back, memorized it, forgot it, and then said it in panic. Now if the moon had helped you, *that* would be strange."

Vanessa nodded, but she was sure she had not read this prayer before. She stared at the words she had written on the folded piece of paper. Why had she prayed to the moon to protect her?

CHAPTER SEVEN

SATURDAY, VANESSA waited impatiently outside her house for Michael. She wore a pale green sundress and sandals that she had bought with her mother in a boutique on Robertson Boulevard. Her mother had been thrilled she had wanted to shop with her. Now Vanessa worried the dress looked too desperate, with its thin straps, bare back, and short skirt.

Too bad, she decided. Why was she so worried, anyway? She enjoyed the silky run of material over her skin.

The sun's last fiery rays dusted the tops of the palm trees with gold as a Volkswagen bus painted with psychedelic pink-and-orange flowers like an old hippie van turned onto her street. The headlights came on, and the van drove slowly toward her. The van stopped in front of her and Michael leaned out the window.

"Hi," he said with a slow, lazy smile. She felt herself getting lost in that smile, those eyes and lips.

"Hi." Her molecules buzzed slow and easy.

He turned off the engine, crawled out, and walked around to the passenger side door.

"You like the van? My dad couldn't part with it, so he saved it for me," he said and opened the van door.

"Nice." She admired it, but her thoughts were not on the van.

She climbed in and settled nicely, her bare back pressed against the warm seat. Inside smelled of spicy foods and beach tar. His surfboard lay on wadded towels in the back.

He hesitated before he closed the door.

"You look pretty." But his eyes said she looked more than pretty. He took her hand and kissed the fingers, still gazing at her.

Waves of energy rushed through her, stirring her molecules into a risky dance. Her hands and neck tingled. She took a slow easy breath. "Thank you."

The van door slammed.

The thought of being alone with him made an indolent smile cross her face. Her stomach muscles tensed, skin tight. Her nervous fingers were unable to stay still. She grabbed the sides of the seat to steady herself as he got in the van.

"I want to take you to the Hollywood Bowl. Do you like music?"

She nodded and watched him look at her. His eyes said he wanted to devour her. Good, she thought, and pushed Morgan's warning away.

"L.A. Philharmonic," she said as the van pulled away from the curb. She let the wind rush through her hair.

A purple crystal hung from a black satin string draped over the rearview mirror. Vanessa touched it. It felt oddly smooth and then it almost seemed to move in her hand. She pulled her hand back.

"It feels alive, doesn't it?"

She nodded.

"It was a gift from my grandfather," he said, and seemed pleased she had noticed it. "It's for courage and patience. A patient heart needs courage to endure."

"I wish I'd known my grandfather," Vanessa commented. "It's just my mother and me. My father died when I was five."

"What happened?" He spoke softly.

"He was a stunt coordinator on a movie," she explained. "Something went wrong and one of the helicopters crashed. I remember seeing it on the news, but I was too young to understand it was real. I thought he was just making another movie. I mean, he had taken me to so many movies where he had rolled a car or jumped off a building. And he was always okay. But this time, he never came home."

He waited a moment to speak as if he were imagining what life would be like without his own father.

"My family's a big mess of people," Michael said finally. "Cherokees and Lebanese. You'll have to come to one of our family get-togethers."

Was he planning their future?

"Grandpa tells great stories. You'll really like him. He gets frustrated with me, though, because I don't believe all his stories. They're just ancient legends, but he acts like they're fact."

She .wondered if his grandfather knew any stories about invisible girls.

Michael turned left and followed a narrow winding road into the Hollywood Hills. At the crest of the hill the houses no longer had yards. Front doors opened onto the corkscrew street. He parked the van in front of a sprawling house perched next to the curb and jumped out.

Disappointment blossomed inside her. He wasn't taking her to someone's home, was he? A party? He had definitely said the Bowl. She wanted to be alone with him, not competing with a crowd.

He opened her door and took her hand.

"I thought you said we were going to the Hollywood Bowl?" she asked.

"It's a surprise," he answered. "I hope you don't mind a walk."

She looked down at her beaded sandals.

"No," she lied, and hated that she hadn't worn oxfords.

He took the picnic basket from the back of the van, then holding her hand led her down a tight cement walk between two houses. They squeezed around a line of palm trees and a Doberman panting behind a chain-link fence.

"Be careful." Michael took a step down a rugged ridge, then turned and helped her off the cement slab and into the underbrush. They walked through dense shrubs. Leaves and grass scraped her legs. They continued downhill under houses built on stilts. Then the houses gave way to chaparral and fire road. He ignored the sign that read NO PUBLIC ADMITTANCE.

"My grandfather told me about this place," he said. "Back in the forties, airplanes used to buzz around the Bowl, so they had spotters, guys with powerful binoculars, stationed on the hills to take the license numbers off the airplanes. Grandpa was one. He loved music and that was the only way he could afford to come to the Bowl."

He pulled her through bushes with waxy coated leaves. A swarm of gnats flittered around her face. She tripped and tumbled against his back. She didn't try to right herself. She enjoyed the feel of him, the sweet soap smell. She let her cheek rest against him.

"You okay?" He turned to her.

The tips of her fingers brushed along his chest. She was sure the twitching molecules in her legs were half-invisible now. Too bad. He couldn't see in the dusk. Kiss me, she thought and lifted her face.

He leaned closer. His warm breath touched her quivering lips.

"Come on," he whispered. "You don't want to miss the beginning." He started forward.

"Damn." Vanessa cursed to herself as she waited for her molecules to reassemble.

"Hurry," he called.

Vanessa followed after him. She could hear the sounds of an orchestra tuning up now. Oboes, bassoons, and flutes followed by a lazy rumble of drums. The sweetness of violins filled the night air, bows scraping strings, and finally the lower-pitched cellos joined the song.

"Sounds like we're just in time." Michael

stepped out on a small ledge. A pole flaking with red rust stood on one side of the shelf. He tapped it with his finger. "The spotter used to attach the binoculars to these poles." He kicked away leaves and stones, then pulled a blanket from the basket and spread it.

"It's a perfect view." Vanessa looked down at the white shell-like building cradled in the natural amphitheater. They were perched high above the concrete bleachers in the rear.

"Have a seat." Michael sat down.

She sat on the blanket, stretched her legs in front of her and kicked off her sandals.

"I should have told you to wear your hikers," Michael began. "I just thought . . ." He shrugged. "Normally you wear real sturdy shoes. At least they feel solid."

She thought of the dance and flushed with embarrassment. Had she stepped on his feet? She let out a sigh and wiggled her toes, then glanced to the west. Her breath caught. A thick crescent moon, hanging low, appeared as the last rays of sunlight drew a broad line of orange-red below the indigo sky. To add an exclamation point to the moon's appearance, the music began. *Da Da Da Dum.*

One star appeared, then another as if summoned by the fervent music.

"Okay, ready?"

She pulled her gaze away from the night sky and looked at him. Her stomach fluttered with nervousness. She was actually alone with Michael. How many times had she fantasized about this?

He opened the basket and pulled out three red luminarias. He lit the candles inside. The flames flapped fitfully in the breeze. Shadows throbbed and twitched until the flames settled.

"I love candles." Vanessa didn't know that Michael was so romantic. She was happy that he was.

He placed two plates on the blanket.

She looked at him, surprised.

"Bread, cheese, sparkling cider, and my own tomato salad made with olive oil, garlic, and basil." He pulled out paper plates. Then, a little embarrassed, he added, "I hope you like it."

"I know I'll love it." She couldn't believe

Michael Saratoga had actually prepared a meal for her.

She took in his beauty, there in the candle's glow. The music surrounded her and she wondered if he was going to kiss her.

She lay back, her arms folded behind her head and looked at the unhidden desire in his eyes. She smiled. Anticipation made her skin feverish. Her molecules flared. She closed her eyes and enjoyed the feel of it. The night had taken on a dreamlike quality, and even the evening breeze was gentle and caressing across her arms and legs.

"My grandfather says the moon is the greatest gift from the gods."

She glanced back at the sky. "Why is that?" She had always felt the same way but had never understood it.

"God put the moon in the sky to remind us that our darkest moments lead us to our brightest."

"Never give up hope," Vanessa finished quietly.

"Grandpa says that's what the phases of the moon teach us," Michael said. "The moon goes from light to dark, but always back to light."

A laugh came from the hillside behind her, so soft it was like a rush of air. She felt it more than heard it. Her back went rigid and she sat up with a start.

Michael had not heard it. He still gazed at the moon.

She glanced at the shifting shadows behind them.

"What?"

"Nothing." She looked back at him and smiled. Maybe it had only been a cat's meow, or a rustle of a coyote attracted to the smell of food. She laid back on the blanket.

Michael moved closer. She could feel the warmth of his body radiating from his skin. "Here, try the Kasseri cheese." He placed a chunk of cheese on a piece of bread and handed it to her.

She felt too nervous to eat but took a bite anyway. The rich flavors filled her mouth.

"You really like it?" he said.

She nodded. "It tastes great."

He stared at her lips. Was he staring at bread crumbs caught in her lipstick? Or cheese stuck to her teeth? She brushed her hand over her mouth and licked her tongue across her front teeth.

"And the music?" he whispered.

"All of it. It's perfect."

He was silent for a moment, just looking at her. When he spoke, the words were quiet. "I love it here," he said. "I've been coming up here alone. It's better if someone is with you."

She smiled and nodded. "I'm glad to be here."

"I've always loved music," Michael explained. "If the only thing you got going for you in high school is your looks and your athletic ability, you could be a has-been by the time you graduate. You've got to have something more to pull you into your future. I've got music."

"What do you play?"

"Guitar and piano," he said. "I'll play for you sometime."

"I love guitar music. My father played a little. He'd strum and I'd pretend to be a famous flamenco dancer." She stopped. She hadn't told anyone about that before.

Michael smiled. "I bet you were cute."

She shrugged, embarrassed. Why had she told him that?

"This is great," he said. "I'm glad you came with me. I was afraid to ask you out. I thought you'd say no."

"Me?" She felt a jolt of delight.

He leaned back on his elbow. "You." His voice was soft.

"I was hoping you'd ask me out," she confessed.

"Yeah?" He looked at her intently. "Then I wish I hadn't waited so long."

She closed her eyes. "Me, too."

The music was incredibly beautiful, all flowing notes and joy. She felt his warm breath on her cheek. When she turned, Michael's face was next to hers. She smiled. He placed his lips on hers. Her breath caught, and then her mouth opened slightly as she felt his tongue. Her molecules danced in pleasure and bounded outward. She tried to pull them back, but the kiss was too powerful. The intensity surprised her. His hand slid down her arm. Then he leaned back and looked at her, his brown eyes soft and longing. She felt a little flustered, not sure what she should do next.

She glanced down. Under the candles' glow, her feet looked like dancing dust, spinning to the music. Her legs had a glittery, transparent quality. Damn invisibility. What if he saw? Quickly, she lifted her hand to his cheek and held his face. She wanted another kiss. She concentrated all her thoughts on making her feet and legs whole again.

"Was that all right?"

"Very all right." She wished she had thought of something clever to say. What did other girls say?

He leaned over, and as he moved his hand to place it around her, he brushed across her breasts. She sharply drew in air. Her molecules collided with cold pain that sent a shiver through her body. So Morgan was right.

He jerked his hand back. "Sorry," he said quickly.

He seemed sincere, but Morgan had warned her. Maybe he brought all his dates up here, acting like each was the only one special enough to share this romantic evening. Then he would use his charm to seduce them.

Her thoughts were broken by hard laughter coming from behind her, still barely audible above the music, but definitely laughter this time.

"Your hand was in the way," Michael kept trying to explain.

Didn't he hear the laughter? She hushed him. There it was again. Was someone mocking them?

Suddenly, an irrational fear seized her. She looked into the shadows under the scrub oaks and felt a terrible need to be away from where they were.

"I said I'm sorry," Michael insisted and reached for her hand.

"Let's go," she said abruptly and stood.

He seemed baffled. "Look, it was an accident."

"I know." She scanned the foliage. She wished they hadn't come to such a deserted place. It felt too dangerous to climb back the way they had come, but even more dangerous to stay where they were.

"Are you angry?" he tried again.

"No," she said too sharply. "But I want to leave."

"All right." He seemed resigned. He picked up the candles and blew out the flames.

Darkness gathered around them, thick and complete and alive.

Maybe they could go down the side of the canyon to the concrete seats. Maybe that way would be safer.

"Come on." She slipped into her sandals.

"Don't you want to go to the van?"

She put her fingers to his lips to quiet him. That's when she heard it, a faint rustle of dry grass followed by the snap of a twig. Something was trudging down the hillside.

"Something is there." Michael finally heard it. He stuffed the blanket into the basket but left the food and the luminarias on the ground.

Tuesday night, when she had sensed some-one watching her, she had felt stark fear. But now a new feeling overrode her fear. She felt an irre-sistible need to protect Michael. Where had that come from? He stood a foot taller than she, with rock-hard muscles. He played water polo, surfed, did all the guy things, but she suddenly felt the Amazon stir inside of her, an instinct that had been dormant all these years. She grabbed his hand.

"Can we leave by going down the hill?" Her voice was steady.

"Yeah, but we'll get in trouble. Illegal access to the Bowl."

"It's better than . . ." She didn't finish the sentence. She started walking, pulling him behind her. What he saw as trouble, she saw as salvation. If someone saw them creeping down the terrain and thought they were trying to sneak into the Bowl, the person might alert the security guards, who would rush to meet them. They would no longer be alone.

"Vanessa," Michael whispered. "It's probably a coyote. They're all over the hills. Or a skunk. Some wild animal must have smelled our food, but it won't attack us."

Then why are you whispering? she wanted to say. From the jagged tone of his voice she knew he didn't believe his own words. Whatever ran stealthily in the dry brush was not a wild animal.

Something blundered down the hill, no longer trying to hide its approach.

She jumped in front of Michael to protect him from whatever was ready to crash through the bushes. At the same time Michael bent down to pull her behind him. Their heads collided in a clap of pain. They fell and tumbled down the side of the canyon, scraping knees and palms.

A dried scrub oak stopped their fall.

"You okay?" Michael said and helped her stand. His hands traced her face and arms as if he didn't trust her to tell him the truth.

Her hands stung and her head pounded. She felt a trickle of blood on the inside of her mouth.

"I'm okay," she panted. "You?"

"Just scrapes."

"We better go." She reached for his hand again. He pulled back.

"If we keep trying to protect each other, we'll kill ourselves."

"We're not far enough away yet." Vanessa didn't let him pull his hand away this time. She grabbed it and held tightly.

Something tramped down the side of the canyon above them.

"I'll follow you, then." He let her lead.

She stepped onto hard baked earth and slid on loose gravel. He grabbed her arm and pulled her to him, his body hard against hers. She wanted to kiss him, to feel his hands on her back. But another sound made her wrench free. How had it caught up to them so quickly? She whipped around and stood between Michael and the foliage.

"Come on," he chuckled. "If it's a skunk, you'll be sorry."

The closer they came to the cement bleachers, the more comfort she felt. But no security guards ran to meet them.

She and Michael sat in empty seats near the back. She was sweating, her mind too stormy to let the music wrap around her. She kept turning and staring into the fierce shadows on the hillside behind them, but she no longer sensed danger, not with seventeen thousand people in the audience.

But the evening was over, the magic gone. She wanted to leave.

She turned to say so to Michael. He seemed upset. She felt suddenly embarrassed that she had made him come down to the bleachers the way she had. How could she ever explain why she had needed to flee?

"Great," he said sarcastically. "Stanton's coming over here."

"Who?" Even as she asked she saw a boy dressed in black walking toward them, his hands in his pockets. His shaggy blond bangs hung in his face. He kept flicking his head as if he was trying to whip the hair out of his eyes.

"What a lowlife," Michael muttered.

"Is he from our school?"

"No, he hangs out with a pack of losers in Hollywood."

Stanton was good-looking, but there was something strange and foreboding about him. His eyes were so blue they seemed luminescent. How could she see the blue so clearly in the dark? Her body thrummed, alert and watchful, as if something portentous was about to happen.

"Hey, Michael." Stanton stared at Vanessa as if awaiting an introduction. He sat down next to her. His body pressed against hers.

"I'm Stanton," he said. His gaze lingered over

her body as if she had invited him to look and take all the time in the world. His blue eyes made her wish she had worn jeans and a turtleneck.

She snapped her fingers in front of his eyes. "My face is here." She spoke with deliberate venom in her voice. Another time she might have let it pass, but her emotions felt raw after the trek down the side of the canyon.

Stanton looked in her eyes and smiled with one side of his mouth. He seemed to enjoy her reaction.

Michael stood. "Come on, Vanessa, we have to leave before the crowd." Was he jealous?

"I was just saying hi." Stanton grinned as if Michael's jealousy fed some need inside him.

Michael walked quickly, his face a scowl. Once they were away from the concert, they hiked to his van in the hills.

Michael helped her into the van, then went around and climbed into the driver's seat. He looked at her curiously. Under the streetlight his face tottered between looking angry and seeming frightened.

"Did you feel it, too?" she asked.

"You mean when we were being chased?"

"No, I'm talking about Stanton," she said. "Something's weird about him."

"You noticed it? The way he gets all happy if he makes other people uncomfortable or angry or—" He stopped. Was he going to say jealous?

"Yes." She looked directly at him.

He started the engine. They drove back to her house in silence. Michael parked with a slam of the brakes, then got out, opened her door and walked her up to the porch.

"I better get going." His eyes were dark and intense. Then he ran back to his van.

Where's my good-night kiss? she wanted to scream. She unlocked the front door as his van pulled away from the curb. She didn't turn to wave good night, because she was too afraid he wouldn't be waving back.

CHAPTER EIGHT

THE HOUSE WAS DARK inside and still smelled of her mother's late-night coffee. Vanessa climbed the stairs. A spill of light from her mother's bedroom covered the hall runner. She stopped at the door. Her mother had fallen asleep reading, an empty coffee mug on the nightstand beside her. She walked to the bed. The fragrance of her mother's hand lotion and face creams filled the air. She wanted to curl against her mother as she had when she was a little girl.

"Mom," she said softly. Her mother did not stir. She pressed her cheek against her mother's and let it rest there a long while.

Finally, she took the book, set it on the nightstand, switched off the light, and went down the hallway to the bathroom. She turned the spigots. Hot water rumbled into the tub. Then she caught her reflection in the mirror. Dirt streaked her face, but it was something more that made her stop and stare. Her eyes looked wide, haunted, different. The pupils dilated, the lashes longer, darker. What was happening to her?

She bathed quickly, put on PJ's from the hook on the bathroom door, and hurried back to her bedroom. She started to turn on the light, but caution made her stop. She crept to the window and closed the shutters against the night, then switched on the small lamp on her desk. She looked at her computer and scanned her room to see if anything looked disturbed.

The door to her bedroom stood open. The dark hallway loomed before her. She took three quick steps across the room, shut the door, and locked it. When was the last time she had done that? Even knowing her mother was down the hallway did not comfort her now. Finally, she called Catty.

A sleepy voice answered the phone.

"Can you spend the night?"

"Now? What's going on?" Catty mumbled, her voice still sluggish with sleep. "What time is it?"

"I don't know. Midnight maybe. Can you come?"

"Yeah, I guess," she said. "How am I going to explain it to my mother?"

"Your mother never needs an explanation." Vanessa looked behind her. Why did she feel so edgy?

"I don't know," Catty hesitated.

"Take a cab. I'll pay."

Vanessa waited at the front window, impatiently watching cars drive past her house. Finally headlights turned down the street, and an orange-yellow taxi pulled up to the curb. Catty climbed from the cab. She held a tackle box in one hand and an artist's pad under her arm. Her messenger bag dangled from her shoulder. She wore bunny slippers and a tan trench coat over her pajamas.

Vanessa ran outside and gave the driver fifteen dollars. He waited until they were inside before he drove off.

Vanessa locked, then bolted, the front door. When they were in her room, she spoke. "Do I look different?"

Catty's mouth fell open. "What did you do with Michael? Tell me all about it. Every detail."

Vanessa flopped on her bed. "Nothing happened with Michael, other than I acted like a fool. Someone followed me again tonight. I don't look different to you?"

"You look tired is all. Someone followed you with Michael there?"

Vanessa sat up and cuddled a pillow against her. "I acted like some freaky Amazon woman."

"He saw your true self? So what? I bet he liked it."

"I don't even know why I did it. I felt like I had to protect him. He's probably never going to speak to me again."

"Then you don't want him. Did you see who was following you?" Catty set her bag down, opened the tackle box, and took out several charcoal pencils. She sat on the floor with her artist's pad as Vanessa explained everything that happened, from the walk down the canyon wall to the strange look in Michael's eyes when he didn't give her a good-night kiss.

"We could go back, you know, and see who was following you."

Vanessa sat cross-legged on her bed. "That's not why I asked you over. I was . . . I didn't want to be alone."

"Maybe it's date anxiety. You've never been afraid of anything before. You've only had these strange feelings since Michael started acting like he liked you. Maybe they're panic attacks."

Vanessa laughed. "I don't think you can call the way he makes me feel a panic attack. You think he likes me?"

"Yes." Catty nodded firmly.

"Did you bring anything to eat?"

Catty pulled a glass pan covered with aluminum foil from her bag. Vanessa could smell the rich chocolate before Catty removed the crinkling aluminum foil.

"The dateless made fudge," she said, and handed the pan to Vanessa.

Four pieces were already missing.

Catty looked at her. "Maybe you should tell

your mother. I mean, it could be some pervert or something. Your mom would know how to handle it."

"Tell her I think someone is following me because I can make myself invisible?"

"It's not like you can't prove it," Catty pointed out. "Sit in the light so I can sketch you."

Vanessa sat in the overstuffed chair next to her bed. Catty's pencils scratched across the paper.

"I think we should go back while it's only a few hours in the past and see who was there," Catty declared.

"Yeah, and end up falling down the canyon. Sorry, your landings make it too dicey."

Catty didn't argue this time.

"Maybe I should visit Serena. She might see something in her tarot cards. Morgan said she was good."

"You don't think she can really tell fortunes, do you?" Catty drew Vanessa's hair in long swirling lines.

"You're right. The best thing to do is talk to my mom." Vanessa watched Catty draw her face, pouty lips, the dimples in her cheeks. Catty was too quiet, which meant she had something more on her mind. Finally she stopped drawing and looked up.

"Did you ever think my mother was right?" Catty said finally. "Maybe we did come from another planet and the spaceship crashed. That would explain the two memories I have."

"The crash and the fire."

"Maybe we survived both, and the moon is like a guidepost that tells us how to get home, only we don't understand it yet because we're still in a sort of larvae state."

"Great, that's all I need. You mean we haven't grown our green antennae yet?" Vanessa joked. She started to laugh, but then she thought of the changes she had seen in her eyes when she looked in the mirror an hour ago.

"Maybe together our powers can take us home."

"Your mother's theory only works if I was adopted," Vanessa said. "And my mother has assured me with gory descriptions of ten ugly hours of labor and twenty-two stitches that I was not."

"But what if—" Catty stopped drawing. "What if something happened to her real child?"

"Like aliens ate it?"

"I'm serious." Catty frowned. "Maybe there was an alien mother who gave birth that night, and a nurse got confused."

Vanessa stared at her. "I look like my mother. You've said so yourself."

"What about the necklaces? Maybe they're like a homing device." Catty started smudging the charcoal drawing with her finger, then stopped and stared at Vanessa. Vanessa knew by the look on Catty's face that she didn't want to hear what she was going to say next. "It might explain who's been following you."

"How?"

"Government agents. The ship might be repaired now. And they're going to send you back to your own planet but they have to make sure you're the right person."

Vanessa thought about it. How would she survive on a different planet? Even if that was where she belonged. "I don't want to leave. My home is here."

"But, Vanessa, if it's true."

"It's not—"

"Just if. If they come for you, don't let them leave me behind." Catty was serious.

"*If,*" Vanessa said. "If it is true, I promise."

"Thanks." She paused a moment. "I keep having this awful dream. In it these shadowy people are trying to reach me. I can't see their faces. I wake up, and it feels so real. Maybe the others are using telepathy to contact us, but our skills are too rusty to pick up their message."

"Stop," Vanessa whispered. "You're frightening me."

"Sorry," Catty said.

"Maybe we should try to get some sleep."

"Okay," Catty agreed.

Vanessa turned off the lights and opened the shutters. She and Catty crawled into bed and stared out the window at the night sky.

"I wish we only had normal problems like everyone else," Vanessa said.

"Me, too. It'd be fun to just worry about school, zits, and boys."

"I worry about that. It's not fun."

"Yeah, it's not fun for me, either," Catty said. "I wish I knew why we're so different."

"Freaks of nature," Vanessa whispered and wondered how she could ever have a boyfriend. Maybe it was better not to try.

"It's hard sometimes," Catty added. "If you weren't here, I'd be so alone, probably smoking pot with Iodos on the back lawn at school."

"Yeah," Vanessa said. "I'd probably be a shy little mouse with a stack of books in front of my face and no friends." She pushed back tears crowding into her eyes. "I'm glad you're here."

"Ditto on the mushy stuff." Catty pulled her covers tight around her.

As she was falling asleep, Vanessa decided to visit Serena tomorrow. It was her last hope before confessing everything to her mother. Maybe Serena could look at her tarot cards and tell her who had been following her and why.

CHAPTER NINE

SUNDAY EVENING VANESSA walked up the tinted stone walkway of a large Spanish colonial revival house. Faded ceramic frogs and trolls sat under the spiked paddles of a prickly pear cactus. The wind blew, and purple-red bougainvillea flowers rained over her.

She started to knock on a large wood door, when it opened.

"Hi," Serena greeted her. "I'm glad you came." She wore Hawaiian-print bell-bottoms and a pair of clogs painted fairy-tale red with blue flowers. She looked like a pixie, the way her hair was moussed with glitter on the ends.

"Let's sit in the kitchen," she said. "The light is better there."

Vanessa stepped inside and waited for her eyes to adjust to the dimness. Then she followed Serena down an unlit hallway. Their footsteps echoed through an imposing dining room that felt cold and never used. Finally, they pushed through a swinging door into a yellow kitchen that smelled of freshly baked cookies.

A raccoon sat on the kitchen table on top of papers that were scattered around a laptop computer. A cello rested against a long counter. Its varnished wood reflected the warm kitchen lights. Vanessa had expected to see anarchy symbols and smell incense, or maybe worse.

"I practically live in here," Serena explained. She seemed nervous to have Vanessa visiting. She picked up a pile of papers. "This is Wally."

The raccoon stood on its hind legs, then climbed off the table and scuttled flat-footed away from Vanessa.

"I got him on a camping trip. His mom deserted him, same as my mom deserted me, so my dad let me keep him. Have a seat."

Vanessa sat down.

Serena went to the counter next to the sink. Wally followed on her heels, his bushy ringed tail in the air like a flag. She tossed the raccoon a cookie, then brought a plate of chocolate chip cookies to the table. "Here, have one. I just made them."

Serena didn't look like the kind of person who would bake. Vanessa picked one, had a moment's hesitation wondering what might be in the cookie, then saw Wally chomping daintily away and took a bite. It was rich and buttery. The chocolate melted in her mouth.

"It's good." She wished she hadn't sounded so surprised.

"I'm glad you like it." Serena smiled. "Sometimes I think about becoming a chef. Well, if it weren't impossible."

"Anything's possible." Where had that come from? She sounded like her mother. Standard Lecture No. 9.

Serena shook the spangled bracelets on her arm. "I guess my life is pretty much planned for me."

Vanessa felt sorry for Serena. Too many kids at school had parents who drew road maps for their lives.

"It's not what you think," Serena added quickly. "Dad's pretty cool. It's other things."

Vanessa started to ask like what, but before she could ask, Serena spoke.

"What do you want to drink? Soda? Coffee? I'm having milk."

"That sounds good."

Serena poured two glasses, then came back to the table and sat down across from Vanessa. She shuffled her tarot deck, then placed it in front of Vanessa. "Think of your question while you divide the deck into three piles with your left hand."

Vanessa took the worn deck and shakily separated it into three stacks. She wondered if the cards would be able to tell her who was following her. When she glanced up, Serena had a peculiar look on her face and her eyes seemed dilated the way Catty's became before they time-traveled.

"What?"

Serena shook her head. "Sorry, I was daydreaming." She took the deck, gave Vanessa a sly smile, then turned over the first card. "Ace of cups. Love affair. Don't worry about Michael. He likes you. It's genuine."

Vanessa tried to smile, but worry kept pulling at her. Did she dare ask Serena about her real problem? An odd sensation rippled across her mind. It wasn't unpleasant, but it felt peculiar, almost like the feeling she sometimes had after completing a difficult algebra problem. She glanced up. Serena was staring at her again.

"You know," Serena began carefully, "if you have other problems, I might be able to help with those, too. I mean, we could ask the cards."

"I've got a problem," Vanessa whispered.

Serena clicked her tongue piercing against her teeth and waited. "You want to tell me about it?"

"I can't."

Serena continued to stare at her. Why did her pupils seem so large? She blinked and her eyes looked normal again.

"Well, maybe the cards can help you if you just think about your problem." Serena turned over the next card, but she didn't seem to concentrate on it—her eyes kept returning to Vanessa.

"Do you see something bad in the cards?" Vanessa asked nervously.

Before Serena could answer, the back door opened. The salty smell of the ocean drifted into the room. A boy walked in, his sandals flapping against the back of his heels. His face was sunburned, his nose peeling, and his lips still had traces of white zinc oxide. Lines from dried salt water traced around the back of his deeply tanned neck. His sun-bleached hair fell in his blue eyes and down his back in a shaggy ponytail.

"This is my brother, Collin," Serena said. "Vanessa's a friend from school."

"Hey," Collin nodded, but he barely looked at Vanessa.

"Hi." Vanessa could see how Morgan would have a crush on him.

"Anything for dinner?" He walked over to the stove.

"Macaroni and cheese," Serena said.

"Where?"

"The oven."

He took the casserole from the oven. Steam rose into his face. Collin set the casserole on a trivet, then took a spoon from the dishwasher and dug in.

"It's hot," Serena called out.

He bit anyway. "Hot!" he yelped, and danced around. Wally scampered under the table.

"Collin's a surfer," Serena said adoringly, as if that explained everything.

"The macaroni is great," Collin yelled. He scooped some onto a plate and left the kitchen. The sound of MTV came from someplace deep in the house.

Serena turned back to Vanessa. "He's pretty cool for a brother, actually. Morgan had a big crush on him for a while. But I think she's had a crush on everyone, especially Michael."

Vanessa sighed and wondered if she even had a right to date Michael. After all, Morgan was her friend and—

"Don't worry about it." Serena interrupted her thoughts. "Collin says Morgan doesn't have boyfriends, she takes prisoners. She's really possessive. So maybe she didn't have a relationship with Michael like she thinks she did."

Vanessa still felt bad. Had Michael taken advantage of Morgan? Was she too embarrassed to tell Vanessa everything about it? Maybe Michael had—

"She never had a real date with him." Serena spoke in a soothing voice. "She saw him at a party and they got together."

"How do you know so much?"

"I listen." Serena smiled. She shuffled the cards. "Let's start again. Think of your question. You need to be specific for the cards to work."

"Okay," Vanessa said.

"Ready?" Serena snapped the cards. "Divide the deck into three stacks again."

Vanessa nodded and thought, Am I in danger of having my secret discovered? Then she divided the cards into three stacks.

Serena gazed at her, her green eyes fiery. Again Vanessa had an odd feeling, this time like a whisper of wind roving around her mind. It was relaxing. She started to close her eyes.

Serena slapped the first card on the table.

Vanessa opened her eyes with a start.

"The knight of cups," Serena said. "He's always a bearer of important news or an invitation to social events." She grinned. "He also brings new developments in love. Are you sure you're not thinking about Michael?"

"Yes." Vanessa tried to concentrate on the two different nights when she felt as if someone had been following her.

"Maybe you should be more specific."

"How would you know if I was specific or not?" Vanessa asked.

"I can't know." Serena giggled. "Just in general people aren't very specific. It's easier for the cards to work if you add in all the details."

Vanessa shrugged and thought of the night with Michael at the Bowl; then she looked at Serena and stopped. Serena's pupils were enlarged again, and she was staring. Vanessa winced. That feeling in her mind was strong this time. Maybe she was getting a migraine. She rubbed her temples.

An odd look gathered on Serena's face as if she saw something that amazed and puzzled her.

"What do you see?" Vanessa asked, the balls of her fingers working her scalp.

"Nothing," Serena said; but her voice filled with wonder and she seemed excited about something. Then she turned the next card. "Damn," she muttered, and her mood seemed suddenly dark.

The card showed the image of a moon with the face of a woman. Two yellow dogs barked at the night sky.

"I think this one was out of order." She started to push the card back into the deck. "Let's go to the next."

Vanessa grabbed her hand and took the card. "What does it mean?" she said nervously. She didn't really believe in fortune-telling, but it frightened her the way Serena was acting.

"The card means an unforeseen danger. Something is not as it seems." She looked at Vanessa long and hard. "It means you should be cautious. Very cautious."

"Why?"

Serena clicked the piercing in her tongue against her teeth. "It's complicated."

Vanessa waited.

"According to the card, you're looking for answers, and the information you'll receive will be difficult to believe, so you'll put yourself in danger. You'll have confused feelings and not be sure what to do, but you can't run from this problem. The only way is through it."

Serena looked down at the cards. She turned over the next and let out a small gasp. Before Vanessa could catch her, she stuck the card back in the deck. Her quick jerky movement toppled her glass of milk.

"Sorry." She ran to get paper towels. She brought them back to the table.

Vanessa helped her sop up the milk. "What did the last card say?"

"Nothing, I didn't even really see it before I spilled the milk."

Vanessa knew she was lying. She had looked too frightened. She had seen something in the cards. And why did she keep staring at Vanessa? Maybe Morgan was right.

Serena tossed the wet towels in the trash, then came back to the table. "So do you want to watch some TV, or go down to Ed Debevic's and watch them dance on the counter? I love their hot fudge sundaes."

Serena was talking too quickly. What was she afraid of? Surely she would tell her if she thought she was in danger.

"You didn't tell me what you saw in the last card," Vanessa said. "The one that frightened you."

"Oh, that." Serena tried to laugh but it came out sounding fake. "I would have told you all the usual stuff that everyone thinks fortune-tellers make up anyway, about a happy life and all that."

But Vanessa knew she was hiding something. "Are you sure there wasn't more?"

Serena seemed nervous. "No, I'd tell you if there was more," she said. "Come on, let's go to Ed Debevic's. It'll be fun."

"I can't tonight. I promised Mom I'd be home early." Vanessa pulled a twenty-dollar bill from her jeans pocket. She handed it to Serena.

Serena started to take the money, then stopped. "I can't charge a friend. Just don't tell anyone else I didn't charge you. Telling fortunes is a cool way to make extra cash."

"Thanks." Vanessa tucked the money back in her pocket. "I'll see you tomorrow."

"Yeah." Serena walked her to the back door.

Vanessa hurried down the drive to the front of the house, then stopped and looked back.

"Freaky," she whispered. She knew Serena was holding something back, but why would she? Was it something about Michael? Or Morgan? She felt heartsick.

She turned and bumped into a girl with long black hair. The girl gasped and took a step backward. She looked like a gangbanger, in black cargo pants and sport tank. Homemade tattoos covered her back and arm. She was thin with large brown eyes that seemed afraid of something she saw in Vanessa's face.

"What?" Vanessa said.

"*Ten cuidado*," the girl whispered. "Be careful."

That made Vanessa more uneasy than if she had snarled.

"Sure," Vanessa muttered uncertainly and began the long walk home. She decided that she shouldn't see Michael anymore. Her heart twisted at the thought. But that took care of one problem, at least. Then she could concentrate on finding out who was following her and why.

CHAPTER TEN

MONDAY MORNING Michael was standing on the concrete steps at school when Vanessa and Catty arrived. He wore khakis and Birkenstocks. His tumble of black hair curled against a white T-shirt. He waved, and adrenaline shot through Vanessa with a sweet pleasant tingle. What was it about his smile that made her body turn traitor to her mind and crave his touch?

"Come on." Vanessa pulled Catty back the way they had come.

Catty looked up. "Maybe he's looking for you."

"I'm done with him."

The look in Catty's eyes told her that she didn't believe her.

"I'm too embarrassed to see him," she begrudgingly admitted. "Besides, I can't have a boyfriend. There's no way it can work out. I can't even kiss him without going invisible."

Catty glanced back at the cement steps. "If he were my boyfriend, I'd find a way."

By noon, heat, smog, and automobile exhaust had settled over the city. Security guards stood at the front gate checking off-campus passes, but kids loitered on campus. The air was too hot and sultry to walk up to Okie Dog or Pink's or sit at Kokomo's in Farmers' Market. Morgan lounged under a tree, fanning herself with an algebra test and sipping a Big Gulp through a straw. Vanessa and Catty joined her.

"Won't this day ever end?" Morgan said. "It feels like it's been going on forever."

Morgan motioned with her chin at something behind them. "Why is Serena following you?"

Serena gravitated toward them and sat in a shady spot near the building.

"She's not following us. She wants to get out of the sun like everyone else." Vanessa opened her bottle of carrot juice.

Serena wore jeans hemmed with red feathers. FLOWER POWER was written on the front of her green tank top. Pointy rhinestone glasses kept sliding down her nose, and her hair was curled in tight ringlets.

"She'd be pretty hard to miss," Catty said. "We would have noticed her."

The hot day had made everyone restless and kids were starting to squirt each other with bottles of water. Steam rose from the puddles.

"I saw her." Morgan wrapped her hair on top of her head. "She's been hanging behind you all day. Weird little goat. You should say something to her."

"Leave her alone," Vanessa snapped.

"Oh, *please*," Morgan bit back with a spark of anger. "Since when does she need you to protect her?"

"Morgan," Vanessa started, but stopped. It wasn't worth arguing.

"Maybe she's the one who's been following

you," Catty whispered, and unwrapped a peanut butter and jelly sandwich that had melted through the bread. She wrapped it back up and wadded it into a ball for the trash. "It's too hot to eat."

"So how was the big date?" Morgan said. She took a piece of ice from her Big Gulp and held it against the back of her neck.

Vanessa didn't answer.

"I warned you about Michael." Morgan shook her head. "You're not sexperienced. I won't hold it against you. But you shouldn't dive in over your head."

"Why do you keep saying that? I thought the sexual revolution was about choice," Catty said. "How can you hold that against anyone?"

"Give it up." Morgan tossed the ice cube away.

"Well, it does seem like you want to make Michael sound bad," Vanessa accused her. "He was really nice."

Morgan gave her a bitter look. "Whatever." She stood suddenly. "This day is dragging. I'm going to the nurse's office so I can go home. Heat exhaustion." She walked off.

"What's her deal?" Catty said.

"I don't know." Vanessa wondered if Morgan was still upset about Michael.

"Why are you still friends with her, anyway?"

"We used to have really good times together, don't you remember?"

"No. She never liked me, and now she's got to bust an attitude on everyone."

"Catty——" Vanessa had something else she wanted to talk about. Something important.

"Yeah, what's up?"

"I've made a decision," Vanessa said. "Mom doesn't work tomorrow. I'm going to stay home and tell her about . . . you know. Maybe she can help me."

Catty frowned. "Are you sure?"

"I don't know what else to do. Besides, I'd rather she hear it from me than see me go invisible on the nightly news."

"All right," Catty agreed, but her voice was dry with anxiety.

A noise startled them. Serena gathered her books and ran across the hot blacktop. She slipped past the guards at the front gate, and didn't stop when the guards yelled after her for her pass. Kids standing against the chain-link fence applauded her audacity.

"Cool," Catty said.

"Why didn't she get a pass?" Vanessa wondered.

"Must've been in a hurry." Catty shrugged. "Let's go see if a classroom is open where we can cool off."

The day stretched on forever. Morgan was right. It felt like someone had bent reality and made classes twice as long. By the end of the day Vanessa was worn out. She trudged across the empty basketball courts, her sweater tied around her waist and shirt open to the third button, when someone called her name.

"Hey, Vanessa." Michael ran up to her, his face flushed. "I've been trying to catch you all day." He touched her arm. A drop of sweat trickled down his cheek.

She tried to pull her breath in slow even draws. She didn't want him to see her nervousness. She almost made an excuse to flee, but the sweetness of his smile closed her mouth and made her stay.

"I'm sorry about what happened at the Bowl." His eyes drifted to the third button on her shirt, then pulled away. "I was pretty rude after."

She thought he'd be angry about the way she had acted. But he thought he had ruined the night. She wanted to cheer. "I had a great time," she said.

"Yeah?"

She cleared her throat. "I loved the music."

He shifted his books and put an arm around her. When his hand touched her waist, new heat rose inside her, a fire for something forbidden.

"Stanton pushes my buttons," he said as they walked across the basketball courts. "It's like . . . do you think someone can be evil?"

"What do you mean?"

He seemed a little embarrassed. "It sounds crazy, but the guy creeps me out."

"Like how?" she asked. But she couldn't pay attention. Her mind drifted to thoughts about his hand on her waist. What would it have felt like if his hand had brushed over her at the Bowl, and it hadn't been an accident, but invited?

"He pushes me, like he wants to make me

mad. Usually he can't get to me, but when I saw the way he looked at you right in front of me, something happened inside me. At first I thought he liked you, too, but then I knew he was flirting with you because he'd heard how much I like you."

"Me?" Her stomach fluttered.

He smiled, and his eyes said *you*. "The last time I really liked someone, he tried to take her away from me. I figured he was the one who was spying on us. I was so furious that all I wanted to do was drop you off and go back to have it out with him."

"You went back?"

"I started to, then I realized . . ."

"What?"

"That's exactly what he wanted. So I didn't." He guided her away from the bus stop toward the students' parking lot.

"You think he was following us?"

"I wouldn't put it past him," Michael said. "So I acted like an ass. Forgive me?"

"Yes." She smiled. And then they were at his van.

"Can I give you a ride home?"

"Okay," she said. Her heart beat wildly. Was this another chance for a kiss?

He smiled and opened the van door. She untied her sweater and rolled it into a ball on top of her books, then climbed in. The air was tight and hot inside. The plastic seat burned her back through her blouse.

Michael got in and started the van. She rolled down her window and let the velvet breeze cool her face. He babbled on about school, his guitar, and surfing. She sank lower in the seat, listening to the song of his voice. Sweet melody, don't stop.

The van parked and her eyes opened. They were in front of her house already.

"Don't get out yet," he said.

She paused.

"I really like you, you know, because you're so different."

Her heart flipped. If he only knew how different.

"You're so mysterious." His eyes smiled slyly. "I like a mystery to unravel." Then he leaned over. He stopped when he was close enough to kiss her and waited, as if he were asking for permission. She closed her eyes. His lips, warm from the heat, rested on hers, and then he pulled away.

She didn't want him to stop.

"I really like you, Vanessa," he said, his face still close to hers, his breath caressing her cheek, and then he kissed her again. Soft, gentle, sweet. His hand touched her knee. Her body tingled, longing for more. The tip of his tongue traced over her lips. His other hand slipped lazily to the back of her head. His fingers traced through her hair. Her body was spinning. The molecules stirred. She shouldn't let him kiss her again. She did.

His mouth pressed harder. She knew what was happening, but she continued to kiss him anyway. At the last possible second she jerked back and hoped her face wasn't drifting into a whirl of golden light. She glanced in the side mirror. A face stared back at her, gratefully whole and complete.

"You haven't been kissed before, have you?"

"Of course I have," she said defensively. She felt embarrassed; her first kiss had been with him at the Bowl. "Lots."

He only smiled. But she didn't see it. She was too focused on looking at feet that were no longer there, only flecks of gold whirling on the floor mats. She threw her sweater over her legs. The sleeve snapped his eye.

"Ouch." He bent down and held his eye.

"Sorry." She felt like an idiot. "I must be coming down with a cold. I feel so chilled suddenly. I better go." She propelled what remained of her body out of the van. Her sudden movement left him unbalanced. He fell forward.

"Vanessa," he called out.

She turned back for one last quick look.

"I don't care if you've never been kissed before," he said, still holding his eye. She didn't answer because she wasn't sure she could speak. Her throat tickled, and sometimes as she became invisible she didn't have all the abilities she had when she was solid. She dropped a pencil and didn't stop to pick it up. Her hand was missing. She ran as fast as she could, hoping he didn't see the way her body was unraveling into a trail of dust. She darted behind the olive tree in the front yard, then sprinted through the lilies and onto the porch. She flung open the front door. Her arms vanished. Her books crashed to the floor and scattered.

She whirled to the front window and floated there, no more than a sinuous vapor. Anyone looking in the window from the outside would see only dust motes caught in a bar of sunlight. She looked back at Michael, afraid he had seen too much.

He started the van and drove slowly away.

"Good-bye, Michael." The words came out like a sigh of wind. A boyfriend would never be part of her life. Even a kiss was too complicated. She looked down at her hands. They were starting to come into focus now. Gradually, the heaviness of gravity began to pull her back into form.

She was going to spend the rest of the after-noon feeling sorry for herself. Why shouldn't she? There was no way she could continue to see Michael. If only there was a guidebook she could purchase to explain the laws of invisibility. Did such laws exist?

Tears started to form in her eyes when someone grabbed her from behind. Her molecules snapped together with a jolt of pain.

She shrieked, mouth open, until air had drained from her lungs.

CHAPTER ELEVEN

"WHEN DID YOU become a screamer?" Catty asked. "It's such a girlie-girl thing. I think you broke my eardrums." Catty hit the side of her head like a swimmer trying to dislodge water.

"You shouldn't sneak up on me, not with everything you know has been going on," Vanessa snapped.

"Sorry."

"It's not your fault," Vanessa said, regretting her anger. "I started to go invisible when Michael kissed me."

"So you're not totally done with him?" Catty teased with a smug smile.

"It's over. How can it not be?"

"Do you want it to be?"

"No." Vanessa's emotions were a knot of confusion in her stomach. "But what would he do if he opened his eyes and saw a ghost hanging on his lips? He'd probably die right in front of me."

Catty laughed, then bit her lip to stop. "Sorry," she said. "But if you think about it, it does sound funny."

"Nothing's funny about his kisses," Vanessa said. She felt herself go fuzzy thinking about the dreamy way he made her feel. "What am I going to do?"

"Kiss him in a really dark room?"

"You're no help."

"Maybe I am," Catty insisted. "If we travel back to Saturday night, I know I can make a pinpoint landing so we won't fall down the canyon wall. I've been practicing all day, skipping back an hour at a time, then forward a little, then back. My landings are perfect now. I landed inside your house at the exact time you got home."

"That's why the day seemed so incredibly long," Vanessa said, and sprawled on the living room couch. "How many skips did you make?"

"I don't know, twenty." Catty grinned and slumped beside her. "All right, thirty-two, but I wanted to get it right . . . the landings, I mean."

"Next time practice in the night when the rest of us are sleeping. Do you know what it feels like to spend thirty-two hours in classes on a hot day?"

"But you don't have a memory of it."

"No," Vanessa argued, "but that explains why everyone was so dragged out by the end of the day."

"No doubt," Catty sniggered. "Next time I'll make sure you're with me."

Vanessa shook her head. She didn't think she had the energy for that either.

"So let's go back to Saturday night."

"But now it's too far in the past." Vanessa raked her hands through her drooping hair. She needed a shower and a nap.

"I figured that out, too."

Vanessa was doubtful.

"I'll leapfrog." Catty spoke rapidly. Her hands made semicircles to demonstrate the leaps.

"I'll go back twenty-four hours, then another twenty-four hours, until we're there."

"It must consume a lot of energy."

"I'll rest tonight. We'll do it tomorrow."

Vanessa chewed the side of her lip. Her real worry was the tunnel. She hated its rank musty smells and the dizzy feeling it gave her. "Your mom said there was probably a good reason why you couldn't go back more than twenty-four hours."

"What does she know?" Catty shrugged. "She's never time-traveled."

"Her explanation made sense to me." Kendra thought there was some natural law that stopped Catty from going too far into the past because the farther she went into the past, the more likely something small and seemingly insignificant could change the future in big ways.

Catty shook her head. "I've thought about it. Everyone thinks time is like a river. But I don't think so. I think time occurs all at once. We just experience it like a river because that's the way we've been taught to think about it. Really, it's more like a huge lake, all time existing at once. And my skips back and forth, that's all part of it, too. So I'll never do anything to change what has happened because if I were going to, I already would have, so I'm not." Catty thought a moment. "It's safe to go back."

"Maybe it is safe, but I don't want to do it."

"Please. Let's try." Catty jumped off the couch, animated again, and nearly collided with the door as it opened. Vanessa's mother walked in carrying three bolts of glittering blue silky material.

"Hi, girls," she said. "Catty, I hope you can stay for dinner. It's been such a wonderful day. I accomplished so much. Why can't every day be like this one?" She walked through the living room back to her worktable in the kitchen, her heels tapping on the wood floors.

"See, some people liked it." Catty grinned. "So how 'bout it? We'll time it so we'll come up behind the person who was spying on you and Michael." She made wild gestures like she was capturing the person.

"Forget it." Vanessa dismissed the idea. An uneasiness spread through her. "And promise me you won't go back alone."

"Sure," Catty said too easily.

"I mean it. At least let me think about it for a couple days. I don't want you to go alone." Maybe if she could make Catty wait and they went far enough into the future, Catty wouldn't try her dangerous leapfrog plan.

"I really promise," Catty insisted, but her eyes glanced too quickly away. "I've got to go anyway. I have homework to catch up on."

Catty left and Vanessa went back to the kitchen. Her mother was cutting tissue paper. She made patterns for the dresses she had sketched that were hanging on the wall.

"Pretty." Vanessa admired them.

"Where's Catty?" her mother said, and snipped the tissue.

"She had to go."

"Without eating?" her mother asked. "Was she upset?"

"Homework," Vanessa explained. "Mom, you're not working tomorrow, are you?"

"I have the day off. I'll be sewing, but gratefully at home. No more measuring sweaty actresses."

"I thought maybe we could have the day together."

She put the scissors down. "Sounds wonderful."

They ate mixed green salads and poached salmon for dinner. Vanessa wasn't really hungry. She felt like she'd eaten two dinners already. She wondered if Catty was practicing again, or simply nudging time to give herself an extra hour for homework.

Vanessa watched her mother cut the salmon into perfect flakes and spear them into her mouth. She loved her mother, but she wondered if her mother would feel the same way about her if she knew the truth about her only daughter. Would she still sit at the foot of her bed to keep the nightmares away as she had done to comfort Vanessa after her father had died, or would the truth fill her with a nightmare of her own?

"I love you, Mom," Vanessa whispered.

Her mother looked up, startled. "I love you, too, Nessy."

"Well, good night, then," Vanessa said. She cleared her dish and put it in the dishwasher.

"Good night," her mother called after her.

She took a bath and decided to do her homework and go to bed early. By the time she plopped on her bed, she was so tired she couldn't fall asleep. She stared at the luminous hands on her clock. She must have drifted off, because when she stirred again, her room was cold.

She rolled over and snuggled deeper under the covers. As she started to fall asleep she saw the curtains billowing gracefully out from her window. She had locked the window, hadn't she? Maybe a Santa Ana had ripped down from the desert and blown the windows open.

That's when she saw the shadow in the chair next to her bed. It looked like a person. This time, she was determined not to be scared. Finally to prove to herself that no one was there, she reached her hand out from underneath the warm covers to touch the shadow.

Cold fingers grabbed her wrist.

CHAPTER TWELVE

VANESSA JERKED HER hand back and sat bolt upright in bed, staring at the cloudy shape of the intruder. A scream scrambled up her throat and died.

"Serena?" Vanessa cried.

"Sorry," Serena said. Her tongue piercing clicked nervously against her teeth. She moved her head, and in the dim light falling through the window, with her hair spiked and her face shining, she looked like a forgotten fairy from some arcane legend.

Vanessa caught her breath and pushed the palm of her hand against her chest. Her heart pounded as if she had almost tripped over a precipice.

"I thought you were sleeping." Serena's words were soft, like a lullaby. "I was trying to figure out a way to wake you up without scaring you."

"If you didn't want to scare me, why didn't you use the doorbell?" Irritation wrapped in tight coils inside her.

"I had to talk to you," Serena said. "It's really important, and I didn't want your mother to know I was here."

Vanessa pulled the covers tighter around her. "Couldn't you just call next time, or talk to me at school?"

"I tried at school, but I needed to talk to you privately."

"You should have tried harder," Vanessa said, her heart still beating rapidly. Maybe this was what Morgan had been talking about when she said Serena was weird. "What's so important?"

Serena hesitated as if she was trying to find a way to put her thoughts into words. "I'm sorry if I upset you Sunday night."

Vanessa sighed and shook her head. "Believe

me, you could have waited until school tomorrow to tell me that. How did you get in here, anyway?"

"How?" Serena seemed surprised. "Your window, of course." And then she giggled in disbelief. "You mean you've never used your window to sneak out?"

Vanessa thought of the times she had left her room late at night under the steady light of a full moon. If Serena ever saw her do that, the sight would jam her giggles down her throat.

"You have snuck out." Serena leaned close to her. "But there's something different about the way you leave your room, Vanessa."

"What do you mean?" Vanessa asked, and wondered how Serena could know what she had been thinking. And then another panicked thought came to her—had Serena seen her?

"Tell me. It's really important. I need to know." Serena grabbed Vanessa's arm, the fingers icy cold. "What is it about you, Vanessa, that makes you so different from everyone else? I need to know more about your secret."

A sudden fear pushed into Vanessa's thoughts. How could Serena know there was anything different about her? Unless . . . the thought came as quickly as lightning struck. "It was you. You've been following me. Why? Don't you know how much you've been scaring me?"

"No." The word hit in one staccato beat and hung in the air between them. "It wasn't me," she added softly. "And stop calling me weird. I hate that."

"I didn't say the word."

"I know," Serena answered quickly, "but you were thinking it."

"You can't know what I'm thinking," Vanessa said, more to herself than to Serena.

"If I prove to you I can, will you go with me?"

"Where?"

"Just promise to go with me if I can prove to you that I can read your thoughts."

"Sure, why not? Like people can do that," Vanessa said sarcastically, and thought, *A dog has brown spots.*

Serena stared at her. "This isn't fair. I can't do it if you're giving me something that has no emotion attached to it. No content!"

"All right, here's another." Vanessa thought of the number seven.

"You're trying to trick me." Serena seemed really frustrated now.

"I'm not!" Vanessa said too loudly, and hoped she didn't wake her mother. She stumbled from the bed and turned on the fluorescent lamp near her computer. White light flooded the room with a buzzing sound. "I don't want you sneaking into my room ever again, and I really think we should wait and talk tomorrow. We could meet at Urth Caffé after school, okay?"

Serena sat back on the chair, green eyes reflective, and studied Vanessa like a cat.

A jolt of energy suddenly filled Vanessa's head. The sensation confused her at first. She tried to close her thoughts, make her mind blank.

Serena squinted. The feeling stopped. Then Serena opened her eyes and the feeling returned like the slap of a cold wave. It felt like Serena was rampaging through her mind, examining stored memories. Impossible. It had to be a headache, some strange flu, a virus. She was beginning to feel dizzy and nauseated.

"Stop!"

Serena seemed to draw back, although no movement was perceptible.

Vanessa sat on the edge of her bed and stared at her. "You can read minds." But even as she said the words she started to disbelieve. People can't do that, she thought. It's probably the cold and being awakened with such a start. Or she hypnotized me. Why?

"Sorry." Serena licked her lips. "I hope I didn't scare you too much. I had to be sure. I needed to know you weren't a trap."

"Trap?"

"It happens now and again. I get deceived," Serena explained.

Vanessa started to speak again, but the way Serena was looking at her made her words fall away.

"You're in danger," Serena said.

The fine hairs on the back of Vanessa's neck bristled.

"You know who's been following me?" she asked.

"Yes." Serena's voice was solemn. "I know."

"Who?" Vanessa asked. She felt a rising impatience not only with Serena but with herself. How could she believe this? If Serena knew who it was, then it was probably Serena who had been following her.

"I can't tell you."

"Why not?"

"That's for someone else to do." Serena stood. "I'm supposed to take you to her."

"You mean now?"

"Of course now. Why else would I have climbed up the side of your house and through your bedroom window to tell you you're in danger? I could have done that on the phone, or slipped you a note at school. You have to meet someone, and she wants to do it now, before you say anything to your mother."

"How do you know I was going to say anything to my mother?"

"You told Catty at lunchtime." She started pacing, her shoes made a steady beat.

"You couldn't have heard."

"Of course not, I read the thought before you spoke it. Hurry. My friend Jimena's waiting around the corner. We've got a car and we'll drive you." She started for the window as if she expected Vanessa to follow her. She straddled the windowsill and turned back.

"Come on," she urged. "Get dressed. Hurry!"

Vanessa hesitated. "If you knew when I was over at your house, why didn't you tell me then?"

"I couldn't. I had to check first. I had to make sure you weren't one of them."

"Who?"

"Never mind," Serena said. "You'll know soon enough if you get dressed and come."

Vanessa fell back on her pillows.

Serena read her thoughts clearly.

"It's not a dream, Vanessa," Serena told her. "There's no waking up tomorrow. This is happening."

"What is happening?" Vanessa asked. "Tell me."

"I can't tell you. I can only take you to the person who can explain it all to you."

Vanessa stared at Serena, poised on the window ledge like some mysterious fairy. She could go with her. Her mother would probably never know, but there was something else to consider. Morgan had said Serena had a reputation for liking the bizarre, and maybe this was part of it. How could she trust her? Maybe Serena was the person who had been following her. Of course, she would deny it if Vanessa asked her. And even the strange feeling that Serena had penetrated her mind could have been some form of hypnotic suggestion, especially with the way she had stared at her . . . the way she was staring at her again now.

"You need to trust me." Her voice was taking on a gentle, almost pleading tone. "Please."

Vanessa wanted answers. She needed to know who was following her, but still she hesitated. "Can't we wait and do it tomorrow?"

"It has to be tonight." Serena sighed. She stared out at the night sky. "The moon is up. You'll be safe."

"What does the moon have to do with it?"

Serena smiled and stretched her arms. "Doesn't the dark of the moon make you feel uncomfortable? And the full moon make you feel strong? Do you look forward to seeing the moon rise the way some people love to watch a sunrise?"

Before Vanessa could answer, she turned to her, eyes on fire, and said, "I do."

Vanessa hesitated but only for a second. "I'll get dressed."

"Great!" Serena said too loudly.

Vanessa knew it was wrong. She thought she would probably regret it, but she hurried to the closet and yanked a pair of jeans from a hanger. The hanger fell to the floor and skidded across the room. She almost had the jeans pulled on when she heard her mother.

"Vanessa," her mother called.

There was a soft padding of bare feet on the runner in the hallway.

"Damn." Serena quickly climbed out the window as the door to Vanessa's bedroom opened.

Vanessa struggled out of the jeans and kicked them back in her closet.

"Vanessa, what's going on? I heard voices." Her mother walked into the room. "Did Catty sneak over here again?"

"No," she said.

"I told you, Catty can spend the night

anytime, but I need to know." She slammed the window shut.

"But it wasn't Catty!" Vanessa tried to say. "It was Serena."

"Don't lie to me, Vanessa. I know it was Catty again. You two just can't keep running around at all hours of the night. You're on restriction. No Planet Bang tomorrow night or Friday."

Vanessa moaned in protest.

Her mother turned off the light and left the room as quickly as she had come.

Vanessa climbed back in bed and pulled the covers around her.

Outside the roar of a car engine filled the night. The pounding beat of hard music followed. She wondered if that was Jimena and Serena, mission failed, on their way to wreak havoc in some other part of Los Angeles.

It took her hours to fall asleep. Did Serena really know someone who could answer her questions? Or was Morgan right? Was Serena just odd? When she fell asleep, she dreamed of a woman riding the moon across the sky. Her pale hair caught the light of the sun, and the long curls became iridescent rainbows that wrapped the world with love and peace.

"There's someone you have to meet," the woman in the dream said. "Hurry."

But Vanessa's feet were frozen. Shadows seeped into the dream then. Opaque clouds hid the moon, and Vanessa found herself trapped in another nightmare.

CHAPTER THIRTEEN

LEAF BLOWERS AWAKENED Vanessa early the next morning. She dressed quickly in yellow drawstring pants and a lacy camisole over her bra, then pulled on a sheer blouse with dragons crawling down the shoulders. She slipped into sandals with butterflies, grabbed her messenger bag, and hurried downstairs. She left a note on the kitchen counter for her mother. She apologized about last night and told her she had changed her mind and decided to go to school.

Then she walked to Catty's house. She told Catty about Serena's late-night visit while they made breakfast burritos with red and green chili peppers, eggs, and cheese, and drank *champurrados*, a frothy mixture of water, cornmeal, chocolate, and cinnamon. When they were done, an early morning breeze flapped the white curtains over the soap suds and dirty pans in the sink.

"No wonder Morgan calls Serena the Queen of Weird," Catty said. She sat cross-legged at the breakfast counter, still in her pajamas, and twisted the ear on her bunny slipper.

"Maybe she has the answer." Vanessa spooned more hot sauce onto her burrito.

"How can you trust her? You don't even know her."

"She seems nice enough." Vanessa took a bite of burrito.

"You say that about everyone."

"Well, she does."

"Look, Vanessa, everyone likes you because you're so nice to them, but I think this is one time when you should be less nice and not so trusting. What if Morgan's right?"

Vanessa sighed, then tossed the last of the burrito into her mouth. A jalapeño pepper burned its way down her throat. She reached for the *champurrado* to put out the fire. "Get dressed," she ordered. "It's getting late."

"You go on," Catty said. "I'm not feeling well. I think I overdid it with the time-travel yesterday."

"You want me to stay with you?"

"No. Get notes for me, okay?"

"Sure." Vanessa picked up her bag.

Catty followed her through the living room to the door.

Vanessa started to leave, but apprehension made her stop. "Maybe I should stay with you." She spoke over the rising smoke from sandalwood incense that burned near the door.

"Go on," Catty urged. "I'm going back to bed. I wouldn't be much company." She held her head down and stared at the bunny slippers, as if she didn't want Vanessa to see her eyes.

"You sure?" Vanessa said.

"Yeah, go."

That was the last time she saw Catty.

CHAPTER FOURTEEN

VANESSA DIDN'T KNOW how she got through the rest of the week. How could she do homework, take tests, or even flirt and smile with Michael when Catty was missing? The teachers said Catty fit the profile of a runaway. How could they say that when they didn't really know her? None of them did. A policewoman had come and gone. So had a protective-services worker from the county. Each had questioned Vanessa at school and then slapped their notebooks closed as if to say, just another runaway.

On Friday, after school, Vanessa sat on the cement bench where she normally waited for

Catty. The day had been hot and now the smog was as thick as tar, and made sky and trees a hazy yellow-brown. The air smelled metallic. She lifted her hair off her neck, hoping the stagnant air might evaporate the sweat.

The thought that had been pushing at her all day finally entered her mind. Catty wasn't powerful enough to leapfrog a week into the past. If she had successfully made the journey back, then Vanessa wouldn't be sitting here in the sticky air. She'd be back at the Bowl reliving her date with Michael. Catty wasn't coming back because she couldn't. Vanessa had a sudden flash of Catty floating in the tunnel, unable to break free.

She heard footsteps and looked up. Michael walked toward her.

"I heard Catty still hasn't come back," he said. "Are you okay?"

She shook her head. "We've been best friends for so long I can't even believe all the ways I miss her."

He sat down beside her and his arm circled her back. "Do you want me to give you a ride over to Catty's house just in case she's come back?"

"Thanks."

She picked up her messenger bag, and they drove over to Catty's house. No one answered the front door. She and Michael went around to the backyard. Wind chimes and hummingbird feeders hung from the eaves, and pink oleander blossoms brushed lazily against the redwood fence. She crossed the patio and knocked on the sliding glass door, then held her hands around her eyes and peered inside. The sun set behind her and the last rays colored the dining room with fire.

They walked back to the van, holding hands.

"I wanted to take you to Planet Bang tonight," Michael said, "but I didn't know if you'd want to go."

"I'm grounded. My mother won't let me tonight, but even if she said it was okay, I'd feel funny going out, not knowing where Catty is."

"I thought that's what you'd say, but I wanted to ask anyway." He didn't hide the disappointment in his voice. "Come on, I'll give you a ride home."

"I promised I'd meet Morgan at Urth."

"I'll give you a ride."

"Thanks, but I need—"

"Time alone." Michael put both arms around her. "Catty didn't like rules much. I think she's run away. Maybe she didn't tell you because she didn't want you to talk her out of it." His tone implied that Catty wasn't coming back. "I'm sorry."

"I know," she said. She was grateful for the understanding she saw in his eyes.

"If you change your mind and your mom will let you go out, then give me a call, okay?"

"Yes."

"Promise?"

"I promise." She smiled. Michael made her feel so good.

He climbed in his van and she watched him drive away. Then she walked over to the Urth Caffé near the Bodhi Tree book store.

Morgan sat alone at a small table near the window. She sipped tea from a huge cup. The steam curled around her face.

"Hi." Vanessa sat down.

"Any luck finding Catty?" Morgan said. She took another sip of tea.

"No. She wasn't home."

"She wasn't at the rose garden at Exposition Park either."

Vanessa must have looked surprised, because Morgan answered her. "Well, I thought maybe she had boy trouble and went someplace to think." She shrugged. "I ditched afternoon classes and took the bus. I like to go there."

Vanessa wondered if she had gone there to think about Michael. She didn't think she really went there looking for Catty.

Morgan stared at her hands. "I can't believe her mother didn't even call the police. That's so like Catty's mother."

"The school called them." Vanessa spoke defensively. Catty's mother had probably driven over to Griffith Observatory again this evening to see if she could spot a spaceship and wave good-bye to her daughter.

"We should do something." Morgan caught Vanessa's look and shrugged. "So maybe I didn't like Catty, but I hate what's happened to her. I'd want everyone to keep trying to find me."

Serena walked into the cafe. She was wearing gold platform shoes and overalls spray-painted with graffiti. Serena saw them, waved, and came toward their table.

"Why is she always following you?" Morgan said, exasperated. "You'd better watch out for her."

"Hi," Serena greeted them. "I was just picking up some books at the Bodhi Tree. I'm glad I saw you here. I've been trying to catch you all week, Vanessa."

"I've got to go." Morgan stood abruptly. "If I'm going to Planet Bang tonight, I've got to buy something to wear." She gathered up her things.

"Bye, Morgan," Serena said.

Morgan ignored her and hurried out.

"I heard about Catty." Serena sat down. "Is Catty different like you? She is, isn't she?"

"Look, I'm feeling really bad right now about—" Vanessa stopped. She had almost said "about losing a friend." The words felt too final to say. She thought of Catty spinning down the tunnel for eternity. Hot tears rimmed her eyes.

"You didn't lose her," Serena comforted Vanessa. "I hope not yet, anyway—if you'll come with me, maybe my friend can help."

"I'm sorry you think this is another chance for a practical joke," Vanessa spat out. All she could think about was Catty caught in the tunnel. She pushed back her chair, grabbed her bag, and walked to the door.

Serena's heavy platforms clumped on the wood floor behind her.

"If Catty were my friend and someone told me they knew someone who could help, I wouldn't hesitate," Serena called out.

Vanessa paused, chewing on the side of her cheek. Serena was right. She didn't have a choice. She had to go with Serena if there was any chance the person she knew could help bring Catty back.

"All right," Vanessa said, but she still felt unsure.

Serena smiled broadly. "Jimena is parked down the street."

They walked across the small parking lot, then down the block. A blast of music filled the night and made her heart vibrate with the beat. The music came from a blue-and-white '81 Oldsmobile. The girl she had seen in front of Serena's house on Sunday night leaned against the car. The wind whirled her black hair around her face. She wore Daisy Dukes, athletic shoes, and a fuchsia T-shirt. Her long dark legs were crossed in front of her.

Serena opened the car door on the passenger side. "Jimena, this is Vanessa. Vanessa, Jimena."

"Hey," Jimena called.

"Is she going to drive?" Vanessa asked over the music.

"Sure," Serena said.

"She looks kind of young to be driving," Vanessa said nervously.

"Jimena's fifteen. Her brother lets us borrow his car."

"You got to know how to drive if you're going to jack cars," Jimena said with a wry smile and climbed inside.

Vanessa hesitated.

"Come on, I quit the life," Jimena yelled back at her. *"Te lo juro."*

Vanessa thought of Catty. She really had no choice. She threw her bag in the back and crawled in after it. Serena climbed in the front.

Jimena started the engine. The sound of the

mufflers thundered off the road and shattered the night. The car shrieked around the corner and the rear end fishtailed.

Serena and Jimena squealed with joy.

Vanessa wished she had listened to Morgan now. She rubbed her forehead. What was the world coming to when Morgan was offering good advice?

The traffic light ahead turned yellow, then red. Jimena blasted through the intersection as the oncoming traffic started to move. Horns honked. Tires skidded.

"We almost had an accident," Vanessa shouted above the music, and yanked her seat belt into place with a snap of metal.

"The light was yellow." Jimena floored the accelerator. The driver of a Jeep honked at her and a woman in a Corvette leaned out her window and screamed profanities.

"Aren't you afraid of getting stopped by the police?"

"In Los Angeles? Who are the *placas* gonna pick? Everyone breaks the law," Jimena said. "Besides, I can outrun them."

The awful gnawing in Vanessa's stomach got worse.

"You'll totally get used to this," Serena explained cheerfully.

"No doubt," Vanessa muttered.

"Don't be so scared," Serena said and leaned over the seat. A silver chain fell from her overalls. A moon amulet dangled at the end of the chain. It looked identical to the ones Catty and Vanessa wore. Was it just a weird coincidence? Maybe there was a shop in Venice Beach that specialized in moon charms.

She started to ask Serena where she got the amulet when Jimena slammed on the brakes. There was a terrible squeal of tires. Vanessa gripped the seat and squeezed her eyes, waiting to become a tangle of flesh and metal. When nothing happened, she opened her eyes. Jimena and Serena were both staring at her.

She leaned forward to tell them she had changed her mind, but the car shot out again. Inertia pushed her back with a quick snap of her neck. How had she let Serena convince her to go with them? It only proved to her how absolutely desperate she felt. But overriding all her doubts was a strong foreboding that something important was about to happen that would change her life forever.

CHAPTER FIFTEEN

THE CAR SCREECHED around the corner and stopped in front of a small gray apartment building near Cedars-Sinai Medical Center. Waves of disappointment rolled over Vanessa. She thought she was on the verge of discovering something earth-shattering. She had at least expected a dark alley off Melrose and some threatening punker in five-inch platform boots with silver studs jutting dangerously from leather clothes.

Jimena shut off the engine. The music stopped. Vanessa rubbed her head against the silence ringing in her ears.

Serena opened the car door. "Come on," she coaxed. "You'll like Maggie."

Vanessa climbed from the car. The sweet scent of night jasmine enveloped her. Jimena walked over to the security panel and buzzed an apartment. A loud hum opened the magnetic lock.

Vanessa followed Serena and Jimena into a mirrored entrance. She glanced at the reflection, three girls with nothing in common, an odd combination.

"Who am I going to meet?" she asked.

"Maggie Craven," Serena told her.

"She's retired history teacher," Jimena added.

"How can she help me find Catty?"

They smiled and pulled her onto an elevator. The metal doors closed, and the elevator trundled up to the fourth floor.

"Look, maybe I shouldn't have come," Vanessa hesitated.

"Too late," Serena said.

They each took one of Vanessa's hands and pulled her off the elevator, then walked her down a narrow balcony that hung over a courtyard four stories below. Ivy entwined the iron railing.

Before Jimena could knock, the door opened.

"Welcome, welcome." A thin, short woman smiled. She wore flowing white pajamas that looked like a kimono. Her long gray hair curled into a bun on top of her head. She hugged Jimena and Serena. Then she touched the moon amulet hanging from Vanessa's neck.

"My dear, dear child, I've been searching for you a long time," she said. Her warm, caring eyes looked so deeply into Vanessa's that she thought the woman was inspecting her soul. "You're here now. That's all that matters."

Maggie motioned them to come inside and they continued down a narrow hallway to a living room and kitchen. Candle flames and oil lamps lit the apartment. Simple haunting music of four notes played from a stringed instrument Vanessa couldn't identify.

"Do you like tea, my dear?" Maggie said.

"Really, I just wanted to ask about Catty and then go."

Maggie pulled out a chair. "Sit, please."

Vanessa sat at the small table. The tablecloth

caught the light from the oil lamps and candles and gave the impression that it was spun with gold and silver threads.

Maggie scooped five teaspoons of loose tea into a white teapot. The round face of the pot looked like the face of the moon. She added boiling water from a kettle on the gas stove.

"Milk?" Maggie held up a small white pitcher. She didn't wait for anyone to answer but poured a little into the bottom of each cup.

"Now we'll wait a moment for the tea to brew." She looked at Vanessa in a loving way. "I'm so glad you've finally come to me. I have so much I need to tell you, but where to start? That's always a difficult decision."

"You know what happened to Catty?" Vanessa said.

Maggie smiled at her and set the strainer on top of a cup, poured tea, and handed the cup to Vanessa. She repeated the same for Serena, Jimena, and herself.

Vanessa drank the tea. It tasted of cloves and honey and something bitter.

"This is great tea." Vanessa sipped again. She

hadn't realized how thirsty she had been until she was staring at tea leaves on the bottom of her empty cup. "Now, what about Catty?" she asked.

"More tea, my dear?"

"Yes, please. What kind is it?" She handed her cup to Maggie. Already her urgency about Catty was melting away. She began to relax.

"Perfect tea for the occasion," Maggie said.

In the candle glow Maggie's face seemed to transform. She looked young, and her eyes, something in them looked so familiar. Vanessa blinked. Maggie looked younger still, and her hands were definitely those of a young woman. Why hadn't she noticed that before? She wasn't old.

Maggie refilled Vanessa's cup and handed it back to her. Then she pulled pins from her bun. She shook her head and ran her hands through her hair. Luxurious curls fell to her shoulders. Vanessa could see now that her first impression had been wrong. Maggie's hair wasn't gray, but the pale blond of shimmering moonbeams, and silky. Why hadn't she seen how beautiful Maggie was before?

"There now, has my tea relaxed you,

Vanessa?" Maggie asked. "After centuries of experience I find it works best to give a little herbal tea before I talk the truth, something to help you see with your soul, not your eyes."

Vanessa blinked. The walls had given way and the apartment was a windswept vault dominated with the classical colonnades of antiquity. She blinked again and the four walls of a small apartment returned.

"Tu es dea, filia lunae." Maggie glistened when she spoke, as if an aura of pure luminosity curled around her. The words seemed similar in cadence to the words Vanessa had spoken when she was being chased.

"What language is that?" Vanessa said in a drowsy sort of way.

"Latin." Maggie smiled.

"I know some Latin words." Vanessa tried to repeat the words as she remembered the sounds, but her tongue twisted sluggishly in her mouth. *"Oh, Mah-tare Loon-ah, Re-gee-nah no-kis, Ad-you-wo may noonk."*

"Yes." Maggie seemed concerned. "You've used this prayer?"

Vanessa nodded, feeling bewildered and totally dizzy. "How can I know Latin?"

"You were born with it," Maggie said. "You know ancient Greek as well."

"I'm sure I don't." Vanessa giggled.

"It seems I've found you without a second to spare if you've already been forced to use the prayer." Maggie looked at Jimena and Serena. "It was easy to bring Jimena and Serena to me because their dreams were open. You must have nightmares, Vanessa."

"Yes," Vanessa whispered.

"It happens now and again, but I'm afraid it's not a good sign. It means the Atrox has already discovered who you are and entered your dreams. That's why it was nearly impossible to speak to you in your sleep and bring you to me. Thank goodness Serena found you."

"Did you say something about an Atrox?" Vanessa couldn't have heard her clearly. The tea was making her feel so strange.

"Not an Atrox. The Atrox," Maggie whispered. "The primal source of evil. Since creation it has been jealous of the world of light and tried to destroy it."

Maggie considered the shadows clinging to the corners of the room. "The Atrox is always around, sending shadows like tentacles to be its eyes. Tell me, dear," Maggie continued. "Have you noticed any inexplicable shadows following you?"

Vanessa thought of the unnatural way shadows had frightened her when she was a girl alone in her room, but before she could answer, Maggie lifted her hands. Silver tendrils pulsated from her palm to the corners of the room and scattered the shadows hovering there.

Maggie stared at Vanessa. "To put it as simply as I can, Vanessa, there are evil forces in the world. The Atrox controls them and the Atrox wants to destroy you."

"Destroy me?" she whispered and began to tremble. "Why me? I'm just—"

"*Tu es dea, filia lunae.* You are a goddess, a Daughter of the Moon."

"Goddess?"

"Yes." Maggie smiled. "When Pandora's box was opened, countless evils and sorrows were released into the world. But the last thing to leave the box was hope, the sole comfort for people during misfortune. Only Selene, the goddess of the moon, saw the demonic creature lurking nearby, sent by the Atrox to devour hope. She took pity on Earth dwellers and gave her daughters, like guardian angels, to fight the Atrox and perpetuate hope. That is why you are here, Vanessa, to keep hope alive."

"How?"

"By stopping the Atrox, of course."

"I'm going to fight the Atrox." Vanessa would have laughed if Maggie hadn't looked at her so gravely. "What happens if the Atrox wins?"

"The end of the world as we know it."

Vanessa felt fear spread through her.

"I'm going much too fast for you, my dear," Maggie said. "Sip your tea."

Vanessa looked at the tea and felt a flood of relief. It must be the tea. There must be something in it that was making her feel so strange. Drug dealers weren't all young and streetwise. Hippies aged. The tea must be a powerful hallucinogenic. None of this was real. Hopefully, the effects would wear off so she could walk home. The whole thing seemed silly now.

"There's something in the tea," Vanessa declared. "It's making me see things. It made you look different and the apartment, too. And I'm imagining you saying these crazy things." She started laughing then, but no one joined her.

"It's a simple herbal tea from Tibet." Maggie sounded puzzled. "Why would I drug you when I need to warn you about the Atrox and the Followers?"

"Followers?"

"The victims of the Atrox, the Followers," Maggie explained. "The Atrox steals their hope, sucking it from their soul. Then they become predators themselves, stealing hope from others, trying to replenish their own and feel alive again. But their hunger is never satisfied. They become masters of deceit. They look like anyone, you or me, but they hate the moon because it is a symbol of Selene and represents goodness. Under a full moon, their eyes turn phosphorescent, and even ordinary people can sense their evil."

"So why aren't people aware of them?" Vanessa argued. "If they can see their eyes and sense their evil, there should be squads of police fighting them."

"A woman sees a glint of yellow in a stranger's eye and rather than trust her instincts, she thinks it's her imagination. It's amazing how far people will go to deny what is all around them." Maggie sipped her tea, then continued. "The Followers also hate timepieces, not digital ones, but watches with hands and, of course, sundials. Anything that reminds them of their eternal bond to evil. It won't stop them like a crucifix is reported to stop a vampire, but it will cause them to start."

Vanessa thought back to that first night when she had felt someone following her. Her alarm clock had been turned toward the wall and her wristwatch had been turned upside down. Could one of the Followers have climbed into her room and changed her computer program to make her think it was the crescent moon so she would walk home alone in the dark? It could just as well have been Serena or Jimena who had climbed into her room. Serena had done it once. Why not twice?

Maggie continued, "And they can never harm a person who does a genuine act of kindness toward them. Evil is so unprepared for that. But then, I suppose few people have ever acted kindly toward them."

Vanessa didn't want to hear any more. It was definitely bye-bye time. Maybe Maggie had been a teacher who had gone mental from the stress brought on at school. Perhaps Serena and Jimena had cruelly thought that Vanessa would find this sad woman's trouble entertaining. She glanced at them and felt a chill settle over her. They looked deadly serious.

"Can I use the rest room?" Vanessa asked. She'd use it, then come back, make excuses, and go.

"Of course, my dear." Maggie handed her a candle.

"I'll just turn on the light." Vanessa started to excuse herself from the table.

"I don't have electricity."

"Oh." Vanessa was startled. "I'm sorry you had your electricity shut off."

"The electricity wasn't shut off," Maggie said

indignantly. "I never had it turned on. I don't believe in electricity. I avoid it when possible. It destroys the magic of the night."

Vanessa looked around her. For the first time she noticed the utter lack of electrical appliances; no microwave, no television, no dishwasher or refrigerator.

"Electricity and certain other so-called conveniences have caused modern populations to lose touch with their deeper intuition, not to mention what they can't see. Electricity." She formed the word as if it left a bad taste in her mouth. "In ancient times people saw the magic in the night. The day, too. But today? How many people do you know who can really see? I can't understand why people insist on ignoring the beauty of the mythical world. How many times do teachers say it's imaginary? Or parents?"

Vanessa shrugged, took a quick step back, and stopped. Her knees felt too shaky to hold her. She sat back in the chair with a thump.

Maggie leaned over, blue eyes tense, and spoke quietly. "The greatest strength of the Atrox is that modern people no longer believe the demonic walks amongst us. So you see why it is so important that you defeat it."

"Me?" Vanessa said. "I'm going to destroy it, like vampires, with a stake?"

"Not like vampires." Maggie shook her head. "I'm talking about an evil more ancient than Transylvania's undead. The spirit who tricked Lucifer into his fall."

"You want me to fight that?"

"You have no choice. That is what you were born to do and it is my responsibility to guide you and to help you understand your powers. Your breed is descended from unconquerable warriors. Remember their courage and never dishonor them."

Maggie seemed to sense her disbelief. "My proof, dear, is in your gift."

"Gift?" Something twisted inside her. Her heart beat quickly and she couldn't breathe.

"Your ability to become invisible." It was a statement.

Vanessa felt herself plunging into a whirlwind of emotions. She had always wanted someone to explain her strange ability to her, but she had always thought the answer would come from science; a failed government project, a strange overdose of radiation, some experimental medicine her mother had taken while she was in the womb. She could even accept being from outer space more easily than this. A goddess? Weren't they supposed to be sweet and lovely and make flowers bloom beneath their feet?

Vanessa stood and grabbed her bag. It couldn't be true. It wasn't true. But even as she was trying to deny it, another part of her mind was recalling the shadows and the nightmares. If it were true . . .

"It can't be true," she shouted. And then she ran.

She hurried down the fire stairs and out into the cool night. She didn't believe any of the ramblings about the Atrox and its Followers, so why did a cold fear grip her chest?

"Goddess." She let the word linger in her mouth. She didn't feel divine. She had zits and cramps and worried about people liking her. She looked up and saw the moon creeping over the buildings.

"Mother Moon," she whispered. She felt awestruck. Could it be? But if it were true, if she were a goddess, then that meant the Atrox was also real. And its Followers, were they somewhere nearby? She turned and looked at the shadows hovering around the cars and trees. She had never felt so alone and afraid in the night before.

CHAPTER SIXTEEN

AN HOUR LATER, Vanessa walked into the kitchen. Her mother was at the worktable drawing lotus flowers, vines, and paisleys on a sketch pad. A mehndi cone lay on the table next to a plate of cut lemons.

"Hi, baby, what do you think?" Her mother held up her hand. She had painted her nails bright red and decorated the skin with a black design. "I can't decide if I like the geometric designs or the ones I'm working on now." She picked up a white cone. "Let me draw the new ones on your hand."

"Don't you know how to make chocolate chip cookies?" Vanessa yelled. Her emotions had been clashing inside her since she left Maggie's apartment. Frustration and anger had won and had been building as she walked home. Now her whirling emotions exploded into the room. "That's what mothers do. They do things to comfort their daughters."

"Vanessa." Her mother sounded more worried than offended. "What is it?"

Vanessa dropped her bag and slumped into a chair at the table. All week, she had wanted to tell her mother about Catty. She had planned to several times this week, but every time she started, it felt too much like closing the door to the tunnel. If her mother knew, then it would be true.

"Mom, we need to talk."

"Did you and Catty do something weird again? She's been getting you into trouble since you were both eight years old."

"No, we didn't do anything *weird*," Vanessa said.

"But you mooned—"

"Mom, we didn't do anything."

"Well, it's pretty embarrassing when your daughter has to appear in court because she showed her buttocks in public."

"Mom, do we have to repeat these old arguments again?" Vanessa said with a heavy sigh. "This is really important."

"All right."

"Mom, what would you do if you found out something about me personally—"

Her mother broke in. "There's nothing I could hear about you that would change the way I feel. You're my daughter. I love you."

"Mom, I'm . . . I'm very different from what you think I am."

"Let's talk about it. We have chocolate chip cookies. How long has it been since we ate cookies and hot cocoa?"

"You can't make everything okay with cookies and cocoa. I'm not a kid anymore."

"I wasn't trying to make anything better. I thought it would be nice. We could have a long talk."

Vanessa stood. "Maybe later. I think I'll sit outside." She didn't want to sit around moaning over her problems. She needed a solution. Serena had said she was going to take her to see someone who might help her find Catty. Instead, the visit had added to her worries.

Her mother looked at the window over the sink. The moon shone huge and ivory yellow through the kitchen window. "You've always loved the moonlight. It seems to relax you."

Vanessa looked outside at the moon. "Do you think there is a goddess of the moon?"

"Oh, several," her mother answered.

"No, I mean for real."

"I was answering for real." Her mother pushed back her chair, then walked over to the sliding glass door, opened it, and stepped out on the patio. The night jasmine filled the cool air with its sweet fragrance. "God must have many spirits to help. We call them angels because that's what we learned to call them when we were little. But there must be many divine beings who act as God's messengers. I think there's room for a goddess or more. When you look at the beauty of the moon it's easy to believe." Then her mother turned and looked back at her. "Vanessa, why are you crying?" She gently wiped the tears from Vanessa's cheeks.

"Mom, where did you get this moon amulet?"

"It was a gift from a woman at the hospital the night you were born. I thought you liked it. You wear it all the time."

"You didn't question her?"

"Well, no. She was a sweet little thing and she fussed over you. She said you reminded her of her own child. I didn't see any harm in taking it and it seemed to make her so happy that I did."

"Did she tell you her name?"

"Maybe. I don't remember. What's wrong, Vanessa?" Her mother looked concerned and put her hand on Vanessa's shoulder.

"Nothing really," Vanessa lied. "Just regular stuff, and I'm tired." She wandered into the yard.

"Vanessa, tell me. Something's troubling you." Her mother started after her but stopped suddenly as if she sensed Vanessa's need to be alone. "Don't get too cold," she said with worry in her voice.

Before she slid the patio door closed, Vanessa spoke. "Mom, I'm sorry. I didn't mean to yell at you."

"I know," her mother said quietly, and closed the sliding glass door.

Vanessa sat in the lounge chair near the hibiscus. The milk of moonlight bathed the trees and lawn with pale magic. She leaned her head on the pillow. Tears streamed down her cheeks.

In the gibbous moon's glow, her molecules became restless, urging her to give in, become invisible, and float over the city. She shouldn't. Not tonight. She was too anxious, her thoughts too mixed. Focus was impossible.

Her skin began to prickle. Ripples like tiny waves washed down her arms. Her heartbeat raced.

"Don't," she pleaded. Her body disobeyed her. A chill rushed through her and her molecules began to spread. She glanced at her hands.

"Stop," she ordered. But her fingers refused her command. The tips of her hands became fuzzy. She blinked. She could no longer see fingers or palms, only feel their essence. The clothes next to her body became invisible, their molecules aroused by the forcible change of her own. Then her body levitated, as light as air, the transition complete. She floated to the kitchen window. Her mother sat at her worktable drawing designs she would paint on movie stars.

Her mother turned suddenly and looked out the window. "Vanessa?" she said as if she felt her daughter's closeness. She looked quickly around the kitchen, then shrugged and went back to drawing.

Vanessa glanced back at the lounge chair. Her sandals and blouse were still there, not enough to make her mother worry or wonder. What could she do about it anyway? Her mind was jangled, unable to concentrate and pull the molecules together. She would have to wait until they came together on their own.

She drifted into the night air, rising higher and higher. A breeze carried her as gently as a bedtime song. The moonlight permeated her molecules, bathing them with hope. Catty would return. She felt sure now. She continued on, riding the night air. Maggie and the strange tea party fell further and further into a blur of memory.

She was near Sunset and Vine when a sudden gust hit her hard. She hadn't been prepared for a change in wind. Before she could collect herself and dive for shelter, another rush of air caught her. Her molecules scattered in two directions. She concentrated hard and almost had them back when a blast whistled into her and spun her into a dangerous vortex. A strong uprising wind split her apart.

Cold seeped into every cell. Even with total concentration she could no longer feel all of her body. Toes, knees, and femurs were gone. Not invisible, just no more. Panic set in. This had never happened before.

Wind thrashed and whipped. Another gust slammed her into the palm trees that lined the street. The palm fronds slashed between her remaining molecules and swept them in different directions. Her mind became confused. Her eyesight blurred, then left.

Silence and darkness cradled her.

CHAPTER SEVENTEEN

THE MUSIC WAS FAINT at first. The beat struggled to find her. Had she been unconscious? The music grew louder and pulsed through every cell. Her molecules gathered. The cadence seemed to regulate her heart. It was becoming strong again. Her eyesight returned. She was no more than long thin bundles of cells, but at least now the cells were absorbing oxygen through osmosis. The side of a building protected her from the raging Santa Ana winds.

She hovered, a transparent veil high over the heads of kids waiting to go inside Planet Bang. It was teen night again. She recognized some of the kids in line.

A gust of wind screamed down the side of the building and blew her through the entrance. It was dark and hot inside and smelled of sweat, cigarette smoke, and musky colognes.

She wavered over the freestyle dancers. The strobe light flashed and cut their dance into freeze-frame clicks. The boys stomped close in a savage circle. They shouted their crew name with the beat and waved handkerchiefs to flaunt their colors. Blue lasers swept over the girls on the periphery of the circle, hips rolling in soft, smooth spins.

Club kids stood near the deejay, dressed in outrageous costumes of turquoise feathers and sequined velvet. Couples stopped and admired their outfits. The club kids posed and danced in their private Mardi Gras parade.

Other kids lolled in dark corners, zombied out. They'd probably paid some homeless guy to buy liquor for them in a corner shop.

Vanessa was lower now, eye level with the dance crews. The pulse of the music beat through her. Her feet found the rhythm and she started to dance, close with the girls. She lifted her hands. She liked the heat and sweat of dancing. She followed the lead of the dance crew, hips in line, and thought of Catty dancing with light sticks and Christmas tinsel.

A hand touched her back. She hadn't realized she had become visible.

She turned abruptly. Morgan stood behind her, all smiles.

"Hey, I didn't know you were allowed to come here after what happened last week." She wore a zip-up top, a silver pull ring dangling seductively at the base of her throat.

"I'm not."

"Cool." Morgan grabbed Vanessa's arm. "You're dropping that goodie girl attitude. I like your outfit. It's a Mom-would-die-if-she-saw-me choice." Vanessa glanced down. She was wearing the lacy see-through camisole over her bra. Her yellow drawstring slacks had thankfully made the trip, but she was barefoot, except for her toe rings.

"This place is definitely a blues buster," Morgan said. "Staying home and crying is a waste of time. All it does is make your nose red and your eyelids puffy. Let's meet those guys over there in the corner."

"I'm not staying." Vanessa turned to go.

"Why'd you come, then?" Morgan took her hands and pulled her across the floor. "Your hands are as cold as ice. Why are you so nervous? Is Michael coming?"

"No, really, I've got to get home. I'm grounded."

"That's a new one," Morgan commented. "Then how did you get here?"

"Long story."

"Right, you're checking up on Michael. I know the game. Look over there." She motioned with her head.

Seven boys stood in the dark away from the reach of the strobe lights. The tallest leaned into the flash of white light as if he knew they were talking about him. It was Stanton.

"Any one of those boys could love me to death," Morgan said. "How can there be so many cute boys I haven't met yet? Isn't life fabulous?" Her voice was a little too frantic, like she was trying to chase the sadness away.

"Maybe you should be careful," Vanessa warned. She wasn't in the mood to say hi to Stanton or any of his friends.

"Those boys look like they need someone to tame them. I'd just be doing my duty."

"Morgan, do you ever think of anything besides boys?"

"Sure, clothes and style. I must be doing something right, haven't you noticed?"

"What?"

"Look at how many girls are wearing a tassel of mini-braids like I wore last week. Imitation is the sincerest form of flattery."

"Yeah, if that's important," Vanessa muttered.

"It's everything." Morgan pulled her through a line of dancers to the smoke-filled corner.

"I think I'll start a diet tomorrow." Morgan kept watching. "It'll change the way I feel about myself." She pinched a nonexistent roll of fat on her thigh.

"Morgan, what century are you living in?"

"I'm just trying to get your mind off Catty. I'm *teasing*. You know I don't believe all that stuff I say."

"Then why do you say it?"

"It's expected," she said, and pointed. "There! That one. What do you think?"

Stanton popped a match with his thumbnail and lit a cigarette. His eyes never left Vanessa.

"I think we should go home."

"Because you have a boyfriend no one else needs one? Please. Look at the tall one."

"I know him," Vanessa said.

"Good." Morgan smiled. "That's the one I want. Introduce me."

Vanessa tried not to stare at Stanton, but she kept feeling her eyes drawn back to him.

A girl stood next to him. She had long maroon hair and wore a low-cut black dress. Something in her hand flashed dangerous silver. It was a razor blade. She lifted it to her chest and cut a jagged S, then looked up at Stanton with a coy smile.

She licked her lips and sliced a T into the pale white skin. Blood trickled down her breasts.

No one seemed alarmed. Vanessa felt sick. She barreled through the crowd and grabbed the girl's wrist to stop her from cutting the A.

Stanton took the razor from the girl, his fingers unafraid of the slicing blade. "Cassandra's into blood sports," he drawled, and dropped the blade into his shirt pocket.

Cassandra seemed to hiss and draw back. She stared at Vanessa, then quickly looked away, but not before Vanessa saw the bottomless black deadness in her eyes.

"She's a cutter," Stanton whispered, his lips too close to Vanessa's cheek. "She can't feel, so she cuts herself to escape it."

Cassandra smiled in a dreamy sort of way and patted at the blood with the tips of her fingers.

Morgan pulled Stanton away from Vanessa.

"I'm Morgan," she said, hanging on his arm. "Vanessa's best friend."

Stanton smiled at Morgan, but his eyes returned to Vanessa.

"Let's dance." Morgan pulled him back into shadows, too much desire and desperation in her face. She held her hands over her head. Her hips moved sinuous and slow. Stanton placed his hands on her waist. She looked shyly into his eyes, then her hands entwined the back of his neck.

Another boy with shadows in his eyes hopped over to Vanessa. She was instantly afraid of him. He appeared to be like any boy her age, but there was something creepy about the way he looked at her.

"You're Stanton's friend?" he said. "I'm Karyl." His eyes held frank sexual suggestion and kept returning to her see-through camisole. He brushed an uninvited hand down her arm. His skin felt dry and thin like lizard skin. He stared at her as if there was something Vanessa had that he wanted desperately.

She stepped away from him and bumped into another boy, tall with white-blond hair and black roots. He smiled at her, lips curved in a crooked sort of way. His nose hoops shimmered. The strobe light made his thin face look haunted. He put his arm around her waist, fingers digging into her side, craving.

She slapped his fingers.

He laughed. "Don't you like me touching you?" He touched her again, his hand dangerously bold.

She pushed him away. "Stop it."

He laughed again. So did Karyl.

She hated that they were making her feel so vulnerable.

"My friend Tymmie's got a longing for something," Karyl said. "I got it, too, a real bad hunger. Maybe a pretty girl like you can feed it."

"And maybe not." Vanessa started to walk away.

The boys circled around her, and then Cassandra joined them.

"Dance with me," she said, her body slinking around Vanessa as tight as a cat.

"No." Vanessa tore away from their hands. She barreled toward the dance floor where she had last seen Morgan dancing with Stanton. Karyl hurried beside her.

"You don't want me to go hungry, do you?" he said. "That wouldn't be nice. You seem like a nice girl."

"Get away!" Vanessa ducked under his arm.

He laughed and jumped as if she had blown him a kiss.

She slammed through the throng of dancers.

Cassandra stepped in front of her. Inch-long fingernails cut into her skin.

"Ouch." Vanessa jerked her arm away.

"Play nice." Cassandra let her bloody fingers glide down Vanessa's neck. "Karyl and Tymmie just want to play. So do I. Be our friend."

"You guys are lost in the K hole," Vanessa said with disgust. Planet Bang was strict about drug use, but kids took them in the parking lot. Stanton's friends were on Ecstasy or worse, Special K, the drug from hell.

Then she saw Morgan kissing Stanton. She yanked free from Cassandra and grabbed Morgan. Her zipper had been pulled down to her silky pink push-up bra. Her eyes looked dreamy.

"Let's get out of here," Vanessa whispered fiercely. "I think they're doing Special K. I don't want to stay and see the rest."

"You go on." Morgan looked up at Stanton. "I'm staying."

Vanessa couldn't abandon Morgan. She had a strange feeling that bad things were going to happen.

"I've got to go," Vanessa said again. "You coming with me, Morgan?" She didn't wait for an answer. She yanked Morgan away from Stanton and rammed through the dancers, pulling Morgan behind her.

She rushed outside into the cool night air. The wind whirled around her.

"What's your problem?" Morgan jerked away from her. "I never knew you were so jealous."

"I'm not jealous! Did you meet his creepy friends?"

"So they're druggies. He's not." Morgan shrugged and started back inside.

Vanessa seized her hand. "It's not safe."

She started to say more but something made her look behind Morgan. Stanton had stopped at the door. Now he gazed up at the night sky as if something in the black endless night was filling him with despair. Was it the moon that tormented him? She thought she saw his eyes flicker with a yellow light. It had to be her imagination.

Vanessa took a sharp breath. "Did you see?"

"Yes. He's beautiful, isn't he?" Morgan breathed. "What's with you?"

A hand touched Vanessa's shoulder. She turned quickly.

"Michael!" She jumped, surprised.

"You told me you were grounded," he said, his hurt and confusion barely concealed in his tight smile.

"She is," Morgan replied for her in a flirty way. "Isn't it great she's getting rid of her goodie-girl attitude?"

Michael ignored Morgan and looked at Vanessa. "I thought you didn't want to go out tonight anyway, because you were too upset about Catty."

"I didn't."

His eyes drifted to the entrance of Planet Bang. Stanton waved and smiled maliciously.

Michael glanced back at Vanessa, then back at Stanton.

"You could have told me the truth, Vanessa," Michael said in anger. "I thought you were a good person . . . I guess I was wrong." His words stunned her.

"I did tell you the truth." Vanessa felt desperate. "Things just happened."

"Why shouldn't she party?" Morgan added defensively.

Michael glanced at Morgan, then back at

Vanessa. "I guess I can see what happened." He motioned with his head toward Stanton, then he turned and walked away.

"Michael!" She ran after him.

He stopped and the look on his face made fear cut through her like a jagged blade.

"I didn't mean to come here tonight. I was going to stay home, but something happened that I couldn't control."

"Like Stanton came by," he said grimly.

She turned to Morgan. "Tell him!"

"Tell him what?"

"Tell him I wasn't with Stanton."

Morgan cocked her head and smiled at Michael with her eyes lowered. "Why would I tell him that?" Her hand slid up Michael's chest. "Did you come to dance with me, Michael?"

The music started again and Morgan swayed to the beat.

"Morgan!" Vanessa pleaded. "Tell him!"

"Oh, please." Morgan jerked away from her. "Take care of your own problems. I've got to go." She left, pushing through the crowd.

"Morgan is with Stanton." Vanessa tried

again. "I don't know why she wouldn't tell you."

Michael shook his head. He didn't hide the sadness in his voice. "Have fun, Vanessa."

She hated the hurt she saw in his eyes. A fierce pain spread through her as she watched him disappear in the crowd, but this time she didn't run after him. How could he think she had come here to be with Stanton? She glanced back at the entrance where Morgan stood with Stanton now. She flashed an arrogant smile at Vanessa before she took his hand and went back inside.

"Thanks, Morgan," Vanessa said bitterly.

"Hey." Jimena pushed through the crowd and ran up to her, breathless. *"¿Qué onda?"*

"We've been looking for you." Serena was following after her.

"I got a premonition when you left Maggie's," Jimena said. "I saw you at Planet Bang. Well, I didn't see you exactly, I saw dust sliding down the side of the building, but I knew it was you."

"I was just leaving." Vanessa started to walk away from them.

"Wait," Serena called. "As long as we're here, let's check out the guys."

"I gotta get home." Vanessa kept going.

"Not yet." Jimena smiled. "You have not checked out guys until you've checked them out with Serena."

Vanessa reluctantly stopped.

Jimena spread her hands through her hair. "Smile pretty."

"Why?" Vanessa asked.

Jimena elbowed her playfully. "Just do it."

Vanessa tried to smile, but her eyes kept scanning the crowd for Michael.

"That one." Jimena pointed to a tall guy with a goatee, dressed in an edgy mix of swing and hip-hop.

"He thinks we're hot," Serena said slyly.

"Well, I could tell you that without reading his mind." Jimena laughed. A song ended inside and the deejay started another. The new beat was quicker, louder, and vibrated through them.

"We gotta jump to this music." Jimena started to move.

Serena leaned into Jimena, their hips moving together. People in the crowd stopped what they were doing and watched.

"Come on." Serena grabbed Vanessa's hand.

"I can't."

"Sure you can." Jimena put her hands on Vanessa's hips. "Just move with us. It's like the bunny hop—"

"Yeah, bunny hop," Serena squealed.

"But closer."

"My hottie is looking again." Jimena smiled wickedly. "What's he thinking now?"

Serena laughed. It was infectious. "It's X-rated. Definitely."

"Take it up a notch," Jimena said. "Come on, Vanessa, bend your knees. Low. Yeah, girl. Now you look like a *nena pachanguera*."

"You can do it," Serena whooped. "Feel the music."

Vanessa felt embarrassed and stiff. She concentrated, trying to bend her knees and move her hips at the same time. It was different from dancing with guys. The muscles above her knees ached as they danced lower, then lower still. She glanced up. A crowd had gathered around them. She blushed.

She stopped dancing and pushed through the crowd. Serena and Jimena ran after her.

"We're going to make a hot dance crew," Jimena panted when she caught up to Vanessa.

"You get a premonition?" Serena asked.

"I don't need magic to know that." Jimena smiled again. "Any fool can see. We're *suave*."

Then they both looked at Vanessa with concern. "We better take Vanessa home," Serena said.

"I'll walk." Vanessa spoke quickly, thinking of the last car ride with them.

"No, it's safer if you go with us," Jimena insisted.

Moonlight glittered through the twisted branches of the jacaranda trees as they drove Vanessa back to her house.

CHAPTER EiGHTEEN

SATURDAY MORNING the sun burned through the gauzy haze, and gray sunlight fell across Vanessa's bed. She reached for the phone and punched in Catty's number. When the answering machine clicked on she hung up and climbed out of bed. She trundled downstairs in her pajamas. Her mother was already at work in the kitchen. Plastic beads and sequins were spread across the table.

Vanessa poured a cup of coffee, grabbed a croissant, and stared at the pottery on the window ledge.

The doorbell rang.

"Who could it be this early?" her mother said.

But Vanessa was already at the front door, pulling it open and hoping to see Catty on the other side.

Michael stood on the porch.

"Michael!" She took a step back, feeling foolish in pink poodle pajamas; then she remembered last night. What was he doing here?

"I didn't want to call," he apologized. "I was afraid you wouldn't talk to me on the phone, so I drove over."

"What is it?" she asked, feeling her stomach clench. Was he going to continue their fight?

He smiled shyly. "I was driving away last night and I saw you dancing with your friends."

She thought of the dancing she had done with Jimena and Serena and felt a blush rise to her cheeks.

He seemed to read her mind. "You looked good."

"I looked silly, you mean."

"No, really." He paused. "I watched you leave with them and then I realized you weren't there with Stanton."

She felt a wave of relief wash through her.

"But then I still can't understand why you went to Planet Bang without me. You told me you were grounded."

Vanessa looked down. How could she explain to Michael what had happened? She desperately wanted to say the words that would make it right. She chewed on her bottom lip. Why did he keep staring at her?

"I was grounded. I never planned to go there." She chanced a look into his brown eyes. "That's just where I ended up."

"Because you were still looking for Catty," he said.

"Well . . ." she started, but before she could finish he interrupted.

"It's okay. I understand. I should have figured it out last night. You and Catty were really close. But you should have told me. I would have understood." He looked into her eyes and smiled again.

She hadn't realized how bad she had felt about last night until this moment. Suddenly, she was happy again. Maybe things were going to work out. Her stomach muscles tightened in pleasure and she felt a distinct lightness in her chest and arms as her molecules swarmed in joy. How could he awaken so many feelings inside her?

"I thought maybe you'd want to drive around Hollywood this morning and see if we can find Catty. Lots of runaways hang out there."

She heard her mother's quick intake of breath. Had she been standing behind them the entire time, listening?

"Mo-*ther!*"

"Catty's run away?" her mother said, shocked. "No wonder you've been acting so strange. Why didn't you tell me? Oh, for goodness sake, Vanessa, you really should have. We'll all go look for her."

"We'd probably get a lot more area covered," Michael offered, "if Vanessa and I take Hollywood Boulevard and you look on Sunset."

"Good idea." Her mother rummaged through her purse. "I can't believe you didn't tell me, Vanessa. Why didn't Catty's mother call me? Of course she didn't call. What am I thinking? Does she even know Catty is gone?"

"Mom, please don't start." Vanessa rolled her eyes upward. "Please."

"I'll meet you at Musso and Frank's at noon for lunch. You should have told me, Vanessa. I just can't believe that Catty's living like a street rat. You know she can always live with us."

Then her mother was gone.

"I'll change and be right back." Vanessa hurried upstairs. How could she tell Michael or her mother that Catty was lost in time? They wouldn't find her where they were looking. She slipped into a funnel-neck sweater and spandex pants and ran back downstairs.

She and Michael walked up and down the streets in Hollywood, threading through thick crowds of tourists, gutter punks, homeless kids, and runaways. They stopped by the homeless shelter on Hollywood Boulevard and checked the bulletin board, then went to a drop-in kitchen and back out to the street.

After they had walked a few blocks, Michael stopped in front of the lines of people waiting to go inside Mann's Chinese Theater and turned Vanessa to face him.

"I'm sorry we can't find Catty," Michael said, and kissed the top of her head. His tenderness awakened a yearning inside her.

His arm circled her waist. When he finally kissed her lips, it felt electric. Her molecules swirled like a lazy whirlpool but when the quiver reached her bones the molecules bubbled up and out, faster and faster. She was dissolving. She opened her eyes. Already her hand was missing.

She yanked away from Michael's arms and ran.

"Vanessa!"

What had he seen?

CHAPTER NINETEEN

VANESSA CROUCHED behind tourists placing hands and feet in the cement movie star imprints in front of the theater.

Michael pushed through the crowd after her. "Vanessa, what is it?" Michael reached for her hand. It wasn't there.

She gasped and jumped behind the tourists taking pictures of Marilyn Monroe's imprints. She focused on making her hand reappear. It didn't.

"Vanessa?" Michael called, sounding worried. "Are you all right?" He caught up to her and tried to take her hand again, but she was afraid he'd discover it was missing. She took a quick step back.

Confusion gathered on his face. "What's going on?"

"I just wanted to see Marilyn Monroe's footprints," she lied, and jumped into the cement prints. Maybe if he looked at her feet he wouldn't see her missing hand. She risked looking in his eyes. Big mistake. She could feel her arm dissolving. What was it about him that made her molecules go so crazy?

He looked down. "Do they fit?" He reached for her hand again.

"Damn," she muttered, and jerked away. She ran back to the street.

"Vanessa?" Michael ran after her. "What's wrong?" He placed his arm around her, but she shrugged it away. She couldn't risk his touch. Not now. She could feel the tremble of the molecules in her shoulder, pinging in delight, begging for his touch to set them free.

No, she thought, this can't be happening. Was she going to disappear right before his eyes? She concentrated, *stay, please, stay,* and walked quickly, hoping the physical exertion might calm her molecules.

Michael walked in silence beside her.

Minutes later, they stepped over the chain circling the parking lot behind Musso and Frank's, then crossed the hot asphalt to Michael's van.

He helped her inside and crawled in after her. She couldn't tell from his face what he was feeling.

"Vanessa," he spoke slowly. "I get the feeling sometimes that you really like me."

"I do," she looked straight into his eyes.

"But then you do things that make me think you don't. Why did you run off when I kissed you? And why won't you let me hold your hand?"

"Well, it's just . . ." She sighed.

"I don't think you're that shy . . ."

"No," she tried again. "I'm sorry I acted that way."

He looked away from her. "I guess I made a fool of myself coming over this morning. I should have left things the way they ended last night."

"No, I'm glad you came over," she insisted with rising anxiety. "It's just that when I get really emotional I start to . . . well, I get nervous when you kiss me and I guess I do act strange." She hated the doubtful look she saw in his brown eyes. She could tell him the truth, but would he even believe her? There was no way.

Her molecules had settled now and she wanted him to take her hand and say everything was okay, but that's not what he did.

"Look, I see your mother coming. Maybe I should go and the two of you can have lunch alone."

"I'd really like you to join us."

"Thanks, but I think I'll go to the beach."

She waited, hoping he'd ask her to go. When he didn't, she added quickly, "We could have lunch first."

"Vanessa," he said quietly and she could feel the mix of hurt and anger in his words. "It's just not working."

She felt suddenly dizzy. "I thought you cared about me, Michael."

"I do," he whispered. "But I don't want a

girlfriend who runs away from me every time I try to kiss her. All I wanted to do was hold your hand. Maybe you don't like me the way I like you. It's okay. We can be friends if that's all you want."

Before she could say anything, her mother tapped on the window. "Hey, did you guys have any luck?"

"You better go."

"But, Michael—"

"Go on. We've said enough for today."

She climbed from the van, an achy throbbing in her chest.

"Isn't Michael joining us?" her mother said with a look of concern.

"No." Vanessa shook her head sadly and watched the van drive away.

CHAPTER TWENTY

By the next Friday the loneliness inside Vanessa was as big as a boulder. She missed Catty. Tears had been creeping into her eyes all week and if she hadn't been in the middle of Urth Caffé with everyone hanging around, she would have started crying again. The coffee and muffin smells reminded her of the crazy times she and Catty had there. She tried not to think of Catty wandering in the nightmarish land between times, but the thought came uninvited. She had a painful feeling that she was never going to see Catty again.

She set her café mocha on the table near the back window, then pulled her books and papers from her messenger bag. She doodled on a course outline, drawing the face of the moon. Then she opened her geography book. The words blurred.

Footsteps pounded across the wood floor. Someone jarred the table and her café mocha slopped over the side of the cup onto the map of Japan.

Morgan sat down. Her smile was like morning sunshine. She crossed her legs. She was wearing new chunky-heeled lace-up boots, her thighs golden and slim under a black mini.

"Hey, I've been looking for you," Morgan said breezily. "I'm going out with Stanton tonight, you want to go with?"

"I don't think so." Vanessa was still angry with her.

"It'll get your mind off Catty," Morgan said. "Look, you got to face it, she's not coming back."

Vanessa dabbed at the spilled coffee with her napkin.

"I know you miss her, but she ditched you," Morgan said. "She didn't even tell you she was running."

The disquieting tunnel flashed in Vanessa's mind. "Maybe she couldn't tell me," she snapped.

"Come on," Morgan cajoled. "I'm just trying to cheer you up. It's better to think she ran than to think—"

"Enough!" Vanessa shouted in a burst of anger.

Morgan was silent for a moment, then she held up her slim tan wrist. "Look." A silver watch dangled on it. "Stanton gave me this watch. He didn't like the one I was wearing."

"I liked your old one." Vanessa frowned.

"This one is digital," Morgan said. "He said I had to get modern."

"Morgan, maybe Stanton isn't really the guy you should be going out with."

"Jealous?" That seemed to please her.

"No." Was she? She had never warned a friend away from a guy. Why would she be? She still liked Michael. But she couldn't get rid of the uneasy feeling she had about Stanton. "Stanton hangs with some really strange people and—"

"Quit worrying about me. I like Stanton. He doesn't act like other high school boys. You know, how they have to be tough and have this attitude like they're so cool. He's different—dark and intense like a poet. I've never had a guy write a poem for me before."

Vanessa felt a sudden yearning for Michael. She wished she hadn't ruined things with him.

"Besides, it's nothing serious." Morgan looked down and waited a long time before she spoke again. "I need a guy in my life. I know that's not cool, but I can't help it. How could you understand anyway? You make friends in a snap, you're really popular and you've got the look."

"Me?" Vanessa looked up, surprised. "That's what everyone says about you."

A satisfied smile crossed Morgan's lips. "Thanks. So don't worry about me. It's a waste of time. I've got it all together."

Vanessa sighed. "Be careful."

"I don't need to be." Morgan looked outside. "He's so fine."

Stanton stood at the edge of the back parking lot, wearing jeans and a black shirt, hair blowing in his eyes. He was incredibly sexy in a wild and dangerous way. She could see why Morgan was attracted to him. Maybe he really did like her.

"Yeah, well, gotta fly," Morgan said. She almost knocked into Serena and Jimena as they walked into the café.

"Hey." Jimena walked over to her table. She had transferred to La Brea High on Tuesday. Maggie thought it was safer if they all went to the same school. Vanessa still didn't believe the things Maggie had told her last week. But she liked Jimena and Serena and had started to sit with them at lunch. After school they went to Pink's for chili dogs, Retail Slut to look at punk rock clothes, and Aardvark's Odd Ark so Serena could buy Hawaiian shirts. More than once, she'd had a strange feeling that she had known them a long time. Everything would be so good now, if only Catty were back. Well, and Michael. She wished she could think of the right thing to say to him.

Jimena handed her a roll with pink sugar sprinkled over the top.

"Here, my grandmother made *pan dulce*. Dunk it in your coffee," she said. "It's really good." She pulled two more from a brown paper bag.

Jimena had three dots tattooed in a triangle on the web of her hand between thumb and index finger. She caught Vanessa staring at it.

"I got that when I got ganged up. It's for *mi vida loca*." She smiled but there was sadness in it, then she pointed to the teardrop tattooed under her right eye. "I got this in a Youth Authority Camp. Means I've served time so all the little hood rats will know I'm one tough *chola*. I got caught up again but the judge gave me community service instead."

Vanessa didn't know what to say. Jimena understood. "You don't need to say anything."

Serena set two cups of café au lait on the table, then sat down. Her hair was parted on the side and slicked back, eyes and lips metallic violet. She looked pretty.

Serena smiled. "Thank you."

Jimena laughed at Vanessa's shocked expression. "You'll get used to Serena reading your mind."

Serena's green eyes stared at Vanessa and then she said in a low whisper, "I can't do it all the time, or the way I need to be able to do it, but I'm learning. Maggie's been teaching me."

"For me it just happens. *Wham*, like a brick in

the head," Jimena said, playfully hitting the side of her head with a clenched fist. Then she looked sad again. "The first time it happened . . ." She gazed out the window as if she were remembering something that still caused her pain. "I was seven, playing with my best friend, Miranda. All of a sudden I got this picture of Miranda in a white casket. Then Miranda touched me and another picture filled my mind. She was walking down Ladera Street. A car was going by. Shots fired. I can still see the white flash coming from the gun barrel. Miranda was killed. I saw everything. After that I wouldn't let Miranda walk down Ladera. It meant we had to go a block out of the way every day when we walked home from school."

"But it came true?" Vanessa asked softly.

Jimena nodded. "I didn't go to school one day. I had to stay home because I had the flu. It was around two-thirty, when kids were getting home from school. I heard the shots and then I knew." She looked away and brushed at her eyes.

"I thought I made it happen because of my premonition." She smiled but her chin still quivered. "Maggie told me I was seeing the future, not making the bad things happen. I don't know what I'd do without Maggie, but in the beginning it took me almost a year to believe everything she said. I mean, *goddess*?" She laughed now and the sad memories seemed to fall back into their dark secret places.

Serena tore her roll in two and dipped half in her coffee. "When I was young, I answered people's thoughts. Not all the time, but often enough so people noticed. I couldn't tell the difference at first."

"That must have shocked everyone," Vanessa commented.

Jimena laughed. "No doubt."

"Yeah, I must have really freaked them out. I know it upset my mom."

"Do you know everything a person is thinking?" Vanessa asked.

"No," Serena said. "Like the night you came over to have your cards read. I didn't know you were a Daughter at first. Then I saw your memories. First I was shocked, then I was excited. I couldn't wait to tell Maggie. I knew Maggie had been looking for you a long time. But then the cards started showing danger for you. Could you tell I was flustered?"

"I thought you saw something in the cards that you weren't telling me." What had she seen?

Serena gave her a curious look. "Just what I told you already."

"That I can't run from this problem?"

Serena nodded.

"After you left, we went over to tell Maggie," Jimena said. "She is one cool woman."

"How did you meet her?" Vanessa asked.

"In our sleep." They both laughed.

"I started having dreams about her when I was about five," Serena explained. "Then when I was around twelve she started asking me to meet her."

"Did you go?"

"After a few months I made Collin take me. He thought I just wanted to check out L.A. By then I was thirteen and he had just gotten his driver's license, so he was really happy to drive me anywhere." Serena took another bite of roll. "I didn't think she'd be there, but—"

"There she was," Jimena finished. "Me and

my home girls went to check out the address I saw in a dream."

"I never dreamed about her." Vanessa thought a moment. Her nightmares had always begun with black shadows covering the moon. And the other night she had dreamed of a woman riding the moon across the sky. The woman had said something before the shadows had seeped into the dream and hidden the moon.

"The Atrox must have sent you nightmares so Maggie couldn't talk to you in your dreams," Jimena mused.

"Maybe one of the Followers saw you go invisible," Serena added.

"A woman saw me once." Vanessa spoke slowly. "I was afraid she was going to tell my mother."

"But she didn't," Serena guessed.

"Yeah, 'cause she was one of them," Jimena said.

The nightmares had started after that. Was is just a coincidence?

"You want to go dancing?" Jimena asked. "We'll teach you some more moves.

Vanessa smiled. She admired girls who had enough nerve to dance the way they did. "You'll have to teach me *a lot*," she said, laughing. But suddenly she thought of Catty. How could she go out and have a good time when Catty was still missing?

"Actually, I better not," Vanessa decided. "I need to study."

"It's all right." Serena gave her a sympathetic look. "We can practice when Catty gets back."

Vanessa stacked her books and hurried outside. Tears came, uninvited.

CHAPTER TWENTY-ONE

VANESSA SAT AT HER desk, her geography book open to the same coffee-stained map of Japan. She couldn't tolerate sitting at home another evening knowing Catty was lost, even if it was in another dimension. There had to be something she could do. She wanted to go to the Hollywood Bowl and see if she could find any trace of Catty. Maybe she could find footprints. And then what? Even if she found a print, what could she do? Probably nothing. But the urge to return to the Bowl became greater as the minutes passed.

Her mother had always told her to follow her instincts. Intuition was an infallible guide. She slammed her book closed and crept to the top of the stairs. Voices and strained laughter came from the television downstairs. Her mother must have fallen asleep on the couch. It was late, past midnight. She didn't think her mother would check on her when she finally woke and staggered up to bed.

She went back to her room, pulled on a jacket, wrapped it tightly around her, and opened the window. She stood in the soft night breeze. The velvet darkness welcomed her. It was hard for Vanessa to make herself go invisible at will. Usually the feeling came, and she either fought it or gave in to it.

She closed her eyes. Silky moonbeams from the last quarter moon washed over her. She relaxed and stretched her imagination out to the stars. In her mind's eye she was in deep space, the blackness as warm and soft as a womb, then she came back to her body and again surged upward into the depths of the universe.

One by one her molecules lost their connection to gravity. They detached from each other with soft pings, until she was a gray mist, shimmering half inside, half outside her bedroom window. A cool breeze filtered through her body and she became one with the night.

She floated over the city. Traffic sounds, sirens, and horns seemed as far away as a dream. She sailed on a current of air over the Hollywood Walk of Fame, then caught a breeze up the hill, and hovered over the Hollywood Bowl. The concert had ended and workers were picking up trash.

She focused all her energy on tightening her molecules.

"Please let it work," she whispered.

Slowly she slid through the treetops and fell to earth, a trickle of vapor settling between eucalyptus trees and flat-leafed shrubs. Her molecules whisked together in a maelstrom that made her body sting. She stood, dazed with the pain for a moment, then stepped forward. Her feet crushed over dried leaves. Floodlights from the Bowl made long narrow shadows slant up the slope.

She stepped out on the ledge where she and Michael had sat. She picked up a paper plate, left behind in their haste. Ants crawled over the plate in single-line formation to steal the last stains of food in the paper. She stared at it and wondered if Catty had found it and held it, watching the ants as she did now, before she had fallen into a hole in time.

Something glowed in the tall dry grass near the edge. At first she ignored the sparkle. Then she stepped closer. Catty's watch lay tangled in the grass. Catty would never leave her watch behind. She had to see the hands to know which way she was traveling, past or future. Vanessa snapped the watch on her wrist. Another glint of light caught in the corner of her eye. Her heart lurched. Catty's moon amulet lay in loose gravel, the chain caught on a stone. She picked it up.

A twig snapped behind her. She turned quickly.

Stanton stood behind her, eyes intense.

She started to take a step back and caught herself. She balanced on the edge of the ledge. If she stepped back farther she would plummet to the cement seats below.

"I knew you'd come looking for Catty," he said, his voice as soft as the night.

"I thought you were out with Morgan," she said, trying to buy time.

"Morgan's here," he answered. "You shouldn't worry so much about your friend." He took her hand and pulled her from the ledge.

Her breath caught. With his face silhouetted against the dark, she knew why he was so curiously familiar.

"You?" she said as a cold knot of fear tightened in her stomach. "You followed me that night when I walked home from Planet Bang."

He smiled, eyes fervent. "Yes," he stated simply. "I've always been in the dark with you."

He pulled her closer to him. His head leaned down and he spoke against her cheek. Soft lips grazed her skin. "I can feel your heart racing. You shouldn't be afraid of me." His breath caressed her. "I've come to help you."

"Help me?" She glanced down. Catty's amulet glowed opalescent. Fiery pinks and blues shot into the dark.

"I've come to help you get Catty back."

"How?"

"Next Saturday, during the dark of the

moon, I'll take you to her."

"If you know where she is, why can't we go now?" she demanded.

"It must be during the dark of the moon," he explained.

"Why?"

He looked at her, then his hand gripped the back of her neck and forced her to look into his blue eyes. A black emptiness seemed to be voraciously trying to drag her in. His thoughts touched hers and then she knew. She pulled away. Everything Maggie had told her was true.

"Because my power is weakest then," she whispered in disbelief and wonder. "And you . . ."

"Yes." He nodded. "I am a Follower."

"You have Catty?"

"If you want her back, you'll go with me and surrender your power to the Atrox."

"My what?"

"Do you want me to say it?" he breathed into her ear. "Your invisibility."

She nodded.

"I'll be waiting around the corner from your house at the lost soul's hour."

"Which is . . . ?"

"Goddess, don't tell me you don't know?" He said *goddess* as if it were her rightful name.

Her hands started trembling. "I don't."

"The deepest part of night, two hours before it dawns."

She watched him walk away. The shadows closed around him. Disbelief mingled with her fear. This was crazy. What Maggie had told her couldn't be true, and yet it was.

She started up the hill. She hadn't gone far when she heard whimpering. At first she thought she was mistaken but the sound came again, a definite human lament. She pushed through gluey cobwebs and tripped over something large and soft.

"Morgan?" she whispered.

"Vanessa?" Morgan flicked on a flashlight hooked to her key chain. A tiny beam of light circled them. The air around Morgan felt thick with sadness. She looked as if she was about to cry, and then she grabbed Vanessa's arm and did. The tears fell warm on Vanessa's skin.

"Something's wrong," Morgan finally said

when she stopped crying. "I feel . . . so . . . empty."

"It's all right," Vanessa soothed, her own voice as thin as a ghost.

"I'm cold, so cold."

Vanessa took off her jacket and wrapped it around Morgan. Her skin felt rough with goose bumps.

"Did Stanton do something to you?" Vanessa asked when Morgan had finished crying again.

"Stanton?" Morgan echoed. She brushed her hand through her hair. Bits of leaves and dirt clung to her forehead. She didn't wipe them away.

"His friends—did they do something?"

"Who?"

Vanessa sat down beside her and put an arm around her. "Can you walk?"

"Maybe," Morgan said, but she didn't move. Even the smallest task seemed to require too much effort.

Vanessa stood, took her hand, and helped her to her feet. Dry grass and dirt covered her boots and thighs. "I'll take you home."

She and Morgan struggled up the steep slope. The wind had shifted and Vanessa could smell the salt spray on the damp air rolling in from the beach. She had a strange feeling that something had cut through the air and ripped a curtain between reality and another plane. And she had entered a shadow universe that few people see.

CHAPTER TWENTY-TWO

AN HOUR LATER, Morgan sat at the table in her mother's blue kitchen, a yellow afghan wrapped around her shoulders. Vanessa warmed a cup of milk in the microwave and set it on the oak table in front of her.

Morgan's housekeeper, Barushe, sat in a rumpled green robe at the opposite end of the table, staring at the wide plank flooring. Her round face said she was still trying to cast off the last remnants of a dream. Then she looked at Morgan and her kind eyes filled with understanding. She kissed the gold crucifix hanging around her neck.

"Can you call her parents and tell them they need to come home?" Vanessa asked.

"I'll call them." Barushe nodded and went to the phone.

Morgan sipped the milk. She held the cup with two hands like a small child and looked at Vanessa with a strange faraway stare.

Vanessa left through the back door. She followed the gray stone slabs around the swimming pool. The water echoed the moon's glow, adding gentle ripples to the reflection. She walked through the pool house. The scents of chlorine and wet bathing suits held the night until she opened the iron gate and stepped into the alley.

By the time she turned the corner to Maggie's apartment a line of deep gray pushed against the horizon, lifting the night. Men and women in bathrobes walked their dogs and sipped steaming cups of coffee.

She pushed the security button at the door to Maggie's apartment.

"Yes?" A voice came over the speaker.

"It's Vanessa."

The magnetic lock buzzed. Vanessa opened the door and hurried inside.

Maggie was waiting for her on the fourth-floor landing when the elevator doors slid open. She wasn't disguised as a retired schoolteacher this time. Her pale moon-blond hair curled around her head like a halo. She was more beautiful than Vanessa remembered.

Maggie smiled. "I knew you'd be back. Now, tell me what has happened that made you believe."

Vanessa told her about meeting Stanton and finding Morgan as they walked down the balcony to the apartment.

"Does that mean Morgan will become one of them now?"

"No, she can't become one simply by having hope taken from her," Maggie explained as she opened the door. "The Atrox doesn't come as a vampire does. Its victims must choose to be Followers."

Maggie and Vanessa entered the apartment.

"Unfortunately," Maggie continued, "evil is an easy choice once hope is gone. Without hope, people become desperate to escape the pain. They seldom see the rhythms in their own lives, how dark phases come before new beginnings. The victims seek the evil of the Atrox because anything feels better than the absolute nothing with which they are left. Violence confirms their existence and evil becomes their way of life. They can become very powerful and very dangerous. And, of course, the Atrox rewards their evil doings. Immortality is one gift it bestows. Now, sit down while I get us some chamomile tea."

Maggie came back from the kitchen, carrying a tray with a steaming teakettle and two cups. She poured hot water over yellow flowers in a strainer. "The dark of the moon is a time too dangerous for you to meet any of the Followers. I absolutely forbid it."

"I have to do something." Vanessa had thought Maggie would tell her all the secrets and send her charging back to rescue Catty.

"I know you're concerned for Catty. So am I. But you must take great care. These creatures of the Atrox are strongest during the dark of the moon when your power is weakest." She handed

Vanessa a cup of tea. "They have power to steal your thoughts, your dreams, your hope, and they can imprison you in their most evil memories. During the dark of the moon you won't be strong enough to resist their mind control."

Maggie sipped her tea, then added, "I must caution you—if they can stop one Daughter . . . eliminate her, then the power of all the Daughters is greatly weakened."

"But they already have Catty," Vanessa insisted.

"Yes, so there must be a reason the Atrox needs you," Maggie reasoned. "The Followers are probably holding Catty as a way to capture you. Perhaps, the Atrox has seen something in your future."

Maggie was thoughtful. "I had always thought it would be Serena because her power is so similar to that of the Followers. She can penetrate minds and see things people keep hidden even from themselves. But maybe . . . maybe it is you, Vanessa. Maybe you are the key, the one who will find the way to wipe out darkness permanently."

"Then why didn't they kill me before?"

"Kill you? No, my dear, the key can turn both ways. If you are the key, then you can be used to increase either the powers of the dark, or the light. If you are the key, the Atrox means to seduce you and have your soul."

Vanessa felt a chill pass through her. "How do I defeat it?"

"Simply by being on the side of good. It's water on a flame, when someone laughs or loves or sings with joy."

Vanessa wanted a simple answer. A silver bullet, a stake through the heart, something definite and precise, but could she do that? Kill? She hesitated a moment, then spoke. "I could never kill anything."

"No, of course not, we never use the tools of the Atrox. Violence only feeds the Atrox. The Followers grow stronger when people use the tools of the Atrox to fight. They become utterly invincible then, because you have unwittingly chosen evil as your defense. You are a force of good. You must always remember that."

"But how can I defeat something if I can't fight it?"

"With the power inside you. As a Daughter

of the Moon, you will know intuitively when the moon is full. So take heart, be brave. It will come naturally to you."

"Then I'm dead for sure," Vanessa mumbled. "Nothing has ever come easy for me."

"This month has a Blue Moon, a fairy night. We'll bring Catty back then. I promise. Now run along home and be safe. Take no chances while I make plans."

"But what will happen to Catty if I wait?"

"If they keep her long enough, I suppose she could willingly turn. But you must promise me that you won't do anything."

"I thought I was supposed to save the world from the Atrox?"

"Yes, but you are too vulnerable during the dark of the moon. And this Dark moon is especially bad coming in the tenth month of the New Millennium It is the Blood Moon. Very risky. Promise me!"

Vanessa hesitated. "I swear."

CHAPTER TWENTY-THREE

BY THURSDAY VANESSA was seriously worried about Morgan. She hadn't come to school, and today was the day they were supposed to sign up to decorate for homecoming.

After school, Vanessa stopped at a newsstand on Fairfax. She bought Morgan's favorite magazines and then caught the bus to her house.

Barushe answered the door. She had a strained look of fear on her face. "I'm glad you're here. Her parents can't come home until next week." She glanced up as if she expected Morgan to suddenly appear at the top of the stairs.

"How is she?"

"I'll show you," Barushe said. "Let me get her tea first."

Vanessa followed Barushe to the kitchen. She had fixed a tray with lemon tea and cookies.

"We'll use the back stairs." Barushe motioned with her head as she picked up the tray.

Vanessa followed her up the narrow winding staircase that led upstairs from the pantry next to the kitchen.

At the end of the hallway Barushe pushed a door open with her foot and led Vanessa into Morgan's bedroom. The first thing she noticed was the odd smell. Barushe had placed bouquets of wild mountain thyme in glass jars and strung garlic across the windows and around the iron bedpost. Barushe came from Romania. Maybe she thought Morgan had fallen prey to a younger evil, one for which garlic and thyme were charms.

Morgan lay in bed, a pink quilt wrapped around her in spite of the heat. Her hair was swept up in a knot on the top of her head, and without makeup she looked pale and childlike.

Barushe set the tray on the bed. "A friend has come to see you." Barushe glanced worriedly at Vanessa, then left the room quickly and closed the door behind her.

"Hi, Morgan," Vanessa said, her voice overly cheerful.

Morgan stared at her, eyes flat. "Hi." She turned her head and a strand of hair fell in front of her eyes. She didn't brush it away.

"I brought you some magazines." Vanessa placed them next to the telephone on the nightstand. The red digital light flashed thirty-two messages. That explained why Morgan hadn't called her back.

"You've got calls," Vanessa pointed out. "Don't you want to hear them?"

Morgan shrugged. "Whatever."

A reflection of sunlight caught Vanessa's eye. She looked down. A razor blade sat in the ring holder next to the telephone. She glanced back at Morgan. The covers were too tightly wrapped around her to see if she had tried to cut herself.

Vanessa sat on the edge of the bed.

"We missed you at school," Vanessa tried again.

Morgan didn't answer.

"Do you remember anything that happened?"

"I," she started, and then looked out the window before she continued. "I was dancing and . . ."

"And?"

"I think." She sighed. "I don't know what to think. What does it matter anyway?"

"I want to help you."

Morgan looked at her. Her dull eyes seemed unable to focus. Her hand reached out from the covers for the tea. Thin brownish-red scabs sliced down her wrist.

She saw Vanessa looking at the cuts as she sipped the tea.

"I can't cry anymore," she whispered, as if that explained the marks on her arm. She set the cup down and studied the ragged lines on her skin.

"Has Barushe seen the cuts?" Vanessa's uneasiness was rising. What had Morgan tried to do? Her concern quickly turned to self-blame; she should have come over sooner.

Morgan looked confused for a moment, then

a slow smile crept over her face. "Barushe keeps looking at my throat for puncture wounds." She tried to laugh but the sound came out wrong. "You think that's what she told my parents?" Morgan said. "Is that why they haven't come home? They think Barushe is being hysterical?"

"Why don't you call them?"

"Maybe later." Morgan sighed. "What's the use?"

Vanessa took Morgan's hand. The skin was wet and cold. "Remember when you talked to me about Catty over at Urth?"

Morgan shook her head.

"You said you'd want everyone to keep trying to find you if you were missing."

"So?"

"So I'm going to keep trying to find you until I get you back. I have a friend who might be able to help."

Morgan's eyes shined with tears and her chin quivered, but then her face hardened. Her lip raised in a show of contempt. "No one can help me."

"She can," Vanessa insisted. "Let me help you get dressed and we'll go visit her." She opened the closet door, turned on the light and walked in. The clothes were arranged by colors. Long shelves held shoes, sweaters, and purses. She grabbed a gray hooded sweatshirt and black flared pants and brought them back to the bed.

"Put these on," Vanessa instructed. "I'll go talk to Barushe."

Morgan looked at the clothes as if she didn't understand.

"Dress," Vanessa explained.

"Get my five-pocket carpenter's," Morgan ordered.

"You got it," Vanessa said, and smiled with confidence. If Morgan could think about clothes, she wasn't completely lost. She hurried into the closet pulled the denim pants from a hanger and brought them back.

Morgan took the pants and stared at the brass button, zipper, and tie as if she were trying to recall how to work them.

Vanessa hurried back downstairs. Barushe was waiting for her at the bottom of the stairs.

"I am so grateful you came to see her," Barushe said. "Her other friends——"

"Other friends? Who?" Vanessa was suddenly alert. Morgan was popular. She had lots of friends, but they weren't close friends who would worry about her absence at school.

"Tymmie and Cassandra," Barushe said. "I think the other one's name is Karyl." She made a face like she was tasting something sour. "I don't like them."

The doorbell rang.

Vanessa grabbed Barushe's hand. "Is that them?"

Barushe looked at her oddly. "I don't know. Maybe."

"Barushe." Vanessa was forming a plan as she spoke. "I don't think Morgan should see them."

Barushe was silent.

"I'm going to take Morgan with me."

"She can't leave."

"She shouldn't see them," Vanessa said again, and lifted her eyes toward the door. "I'll take her down the back stairs and over to a friend's house."

Barushe looked uncertain.

"Can you tell them she's sleeping? Please. Give me enough time to get Morgan away."

Barushe nodded but her eyes looked nervous.

Vanessa hurried back to Morgan's bedroom. She took Morgan's hand. "We're leaving."

Morgan looked at her blankly.

Vanessa tugged. "Come on."

Morgan followed reluctantly down the hallway to the back stairs. Vanessa could hear Barushe talking to Tymmie.

"No, she's sleeping." Barushe spoke with a slight tremor in her voice.

"We'll wake her up then," Tymmie replied.

"Like Sleeping Beauty," Karyl snickered.

"I better go see my friends," Morgan said in a dazed kind of way.

Vanessa pushed her out the back door. "Not now."

It was after seven when she finally had Morgan in Maggie's apartment. Maggie didn't seem surprised by Morgan's condition.

She sat Morgan in a chair and stood behind her. "They have stolen some of her thoughts, maybe, but at least she's not imprisoned in their memories. Her soul needs to visit the spirit-world for healing." Maggie gently touched Morgan's hair.

"Can you do that?"

Maggie smiled as if Vanessa had asked a silly question. "People do it every day in prayer. You go on now. I'll make sure she gets home."

Vanessa started for the door.

"Vanessa," Maggie called as she opened the door. "Remember your promise."

Vanessa nodded and left.

On the way home, she looked at her hands. They were trembling. Fear was a mild word compared to what she was feeling. She realized then that she had made her decision. She knew now what she had to do.

CHAPTER TWENTY-FOUR

SATURDAY NIGHT, Vanessa lay curled in her covers, waiting for her mother to fall asleep. She was going to meet Stanton. She didn't see that she had a choice. She had to defy Maggie. What if she waited and something happened to Catty? She couldn't let them do to Catty what they had already done to Morgan. And if they had already? That was even more reason to go now and rescue her. She threw back the blankets and crept down the hallway to the third bedroom where her mother stored the clothing she designed for movies.

She opened the door and walked inside. The room smelled of dust and mothballs. She flicked on a light and searched through the dresses hanging on racks. She held a scarlet sequin dress to her chest and posed in front of the mirror. Too hot. She put it back and took a black mini. Too dreary. Then a blue as pale as a whisper caught her eye. She took the dress. The material was silky and clinging. Perfect for a goddess. On the floor below the dress sat strappy wraparound high-heeled sandals that matched the blue.

She didn't understand why she needed to dress up to meet Stanton but the impulse to steal into the storage room had been rising in her since the sun set.

She took the dress and sandals back to her room, then sat on the floor and painted her toenails and fingernails pale blue. She drew waves of eternal flames and spiral hearts in silver and blue around her ankles and up her legs with body paints.

When she was done, she pressed a Q-tip into glitter eye shadow and spread sparkles on her lid and below her eye. With a sudden impulse she swirled the lines over her temple and into her hairline. She liked the look.

She rolled blue mascara on her lashes, then brushed her hair and snapped crystals in the long blond strands. She squeezed glitter lotion into her palms and rubbed it on her shoulders and arms. Last she took the dress and stepped into it. She turned to the mirror on the closet door.

A thrill ran through her. Her reflection astonished her. She looked otherworldly, a mystical creature . . . eyes large, skin glowing, eyelashes longer, thicker. Everything about her was more powerful and sleek and fairy tale. Surely this wasn't really happening. Maybe she would wake up and run to school and tell Catty about her crazy dream. But another part of her knew this was real.

She leaned to one side. The dress exposed too much thigh.

"Good." Her audacity surprised her. Another time she would have changed her dress. But why should she?

She took Catty's moon amulet from her dresser and placed it around her neck, next to her own. When the two charms touched, silver sparks cascaded from the metals and remained bright stars on her skin.

She grabbed the shoes, tiptoed down the hallway to her mother's room, and crept inside. She kissed her mother good-bye. The kiss remained visible on her mother's forehead, all rainbow and glitter dust.

Finally, she turned, back straight and strong, and walked through the still house and out the front door. She sat on the porch steps and put on her sandals. As she tied the straps, it came to her with a sudden shock. She had been preparing for battle like a medieval knight, or an ancient warrior, with ritual and ceremony.

She stood. She felt ready.

She strolled luxuriously down the dark empty street as if she owned the night. Her heels clicked nicely on the cement walk. She didn't feel self-conscious or fearful that people might see her. She felt good in her body, thrilled to belong in it. She whooped. It was a war cry. The lights in the house beside her flicked on.

Let them peek out their windows and see me, she thought.

Stanton had told her he would be waiting around the corner from her house the night she met him in the hills surrounding the Hollywood Bowl. She felt his presence before she even turned the corner.

Stanton stood silent against his car, his blond hair tousled in the night breeze. The car was sleek black metal, low to the ground, and spitting reflections from the street lamps. He glanced up when he saw her but didn't move. His blues eyes met hers, and she glimpsed something predatory in them.

He took three quick steps toward her. She tried hard to keep herself steady. She didn't flinch. She wouldn't let herself feel afraid. The air between them prickled with static electricity. He smiled and she thought for a moment he was going to kiss her.

"I didn't think you would come." His breath was sweet and warm and mingled with hers.

"I'm here for Catty."

She saw something in his eyes then. Was it disappointment? Maybe it had only been her imagination. He turned as if he didn't want her to look in his eyes and walked away from her, his slow easy steps echoing into the night. He opened the car door. She followed him and started to climb into the car but stopped. She saw her image in the car window. A goddess. Her breath caught, heartbeat quickened. She couldn't pull away from her reflection. It was as if the warrior goddess had emerged, and she looked less human, more dangerously beautiful. Stanton seemed to know what had stopped her.

"That's how I've always seen you," he said. "Since the first night."

Her head jerked around and she caught something in his eyes before they turned hard again. It wasn't her imagination this time. She definitely saw something gentle and caring.

"What do you mean by the first night? How long have you been watching me?"

"Awhile," he smiled mysteriously. He took her hand and helped her into the car.

Her dress was too short and rode up her thighs. Her long legs stretched in front of her, glistening with glitter and entwined with flames and hearts.

He jumped in the driver's seat, then turned the key in the ignition. The engine roared like slow, thick thunder. The car pulled away, and they drove toward the southeast side of Los Angeles. He merged into traffic on the Hollywood Freeway. Headlights cast light and shadow across their faces. They rode in uncomfortable silence, her body too aware of his presence. She took a deep breath, trying to calm herself and glanced at him.

"Is Catty all right?"

"You'll see soon." He cut in front of a speeding car.

"How did you . . ." she started to ask, but her mouth was so dry her words caught in her throat. She had to be braver. Finally, she asked, "How did you become a Follower?"

He glanced at her, then back at the freeway. "You don't need to know"

She took another long breath. "I was just wondering if someone did to you what you did to Morgan." There was too much challenge in her voice. She regretted it as soon as the words were spoken.

He grabbed her hand.

"Let me show you, then." He drew her to him, forcing her to look in his eyes.

His eyes were startlingly compelling. She tried to pull away. She grabbed the steering wheel. The car swerved. A car honked and three cars sped around them.

Against her will, she felt herself pulled into his memories. She struggled desperately, trying to resist the terrible force. Then his mind was in hers, but it wasn't as horrible as she had imagined. He seemed to be holding back as if he were afraid to frighten her. Then his memories flooded into her, coming so quickly they spun inside her, as if he had waited a long time to share them with someone. She clutched his hand tightly. She was afraid that if his hand let go she would remain lost in his memories. She saw a small blond boy hugging his grandfather's tombstone. The same boy running after his mother when she left him in the care of another couple. And the boy waving good-bye to a man in plate armor riding a prancing black horse. The sad feelings associated with the memories overwhelmed her. His fear and grief and loneliness. Then she felt something else. Something she was sure he had wanted her to see. He had been following her that night a month back, but not to harm her, he had wanted to warn her. Of what? He had stopped following her when he felt the shadows of the Atrox watching him.

She could feel his sudden hesitation now, his need to hide those feelings and memories from her. Then his hand let go and she was falling into a deep black hole. She tried to grab the car seat. Her hands swooshed through empty air. There was nothing but darkness around her.

She had been deceived so easily. Now she was lost. What had Maggie said? The Followers had the power to imprison you in their most evil memories.

She tumbled in the black void.

Then she landed painfully on a cold rock floor.

She stood. Behind her milky light fell through a small window in a damp stone wall. She looked outside. A turret was above her, below a moat. The rising stench from the moat waters made her gag. She was in a castle. She must have been transported back in time as well. Is this where they held Catty captive?

The great hall behind her filled with a soft whimper. Was it Catty? At least they would be together.

She followed the sound to a plank wood door. She pushed against the heavy wood. The door opened slowly with a soft groan. She peered inside. Gradually her eyes adjusted to the utter darkness. A small boy sat on a large bed, crying. He didn't seem aware of her presence. His eyes held something in the corner of the room.

She stepped to his bed. Unnatural shadows gathered overhead. Like black thunder clouds, the shadows surged and grew. Was that the Atrox? Suddenly, the shadows swept toward the boy. He shrieked and pulled the covers over his head.

Stanton might have deceived her and trapped her in another time, but she could still save this child. She pushed through the frenzied shadows and grabbed the boy. His body felt cold and thin as bones on an altar. She held him tight against her and ran.

The dark shadows swirled in anger, then

charged after her with a savage whip of air. She staggered. The boy screamed.

"Don't cry," she soothed. "I'll find a way to get us out."

She ran from the room with the crying child down a vast hall. The furor of the shadows shook the stone walls.

At the end of the hall she entered a dark stairwell. The steps were twisting, steep, and narrow. She kept her shoulder against the wall for balance and plunged downward. The boy sobbed in her neck. His tears ran down her back.

The shadows whipped down the stairwell with tumultuous fury, howling like a squall. She tripped and fell. A force greater than she could have imagined stripped the child from her arms. She struggled to stand. Her hands searched frantically in the dark for the boy.

His crying became farther and farther away. Then he was gone.

A demon-dark shadow eclipsed the others. She knew instinctively that it was the Atrox. It seeped into her lungs with complete coldness. She struggled to breathe.

A hand reached through the darkness and grasped hers. It yanked hard.

Suddenly she was back in the car, clasping Stanton's hand. She gasped for air. Had she only been lost in his memory? It had felt so real. What would have happened if he had not pulled her back?

"You tried to save me," he whispered. "That was the night the Atrox took me from my home. You were going to fight the Atrox." His finger wiped a child's tear from her neck and held it in front of her eyes as proof.

"I'm sorry I didn't save you." She kissed the tear on the tip of his finger.

He seemed overcome with emotion. He snapped his hand back and tapped the steering wheel.

"No one could have saved me anyway." He stared ahead of him, but when he spoke she saw a quick flicker of doubt cross his eyes. He seemed to be saying the words to convince himself.

He turned off the freeway into a dark and dangerous part of town. They were in an industrial area. Bleak warehouses lined the street.

"What happened that night?" she asked.

"That was the night I lost who I once was." His voice choked. "Now I can no longer remember the person I used to be."

"But why did it take you when you were just a boy?"

"My father was a great prince of western Europe during the thirteenth century. He'd raised an army to go on a crusade," Stanton said.

"So he left you alone."

"My father didn't go on a crusade to the Holy Land. It was a crusade against the Atrox. The Atrox knew that by taking me, it could stop my father."

Without being aware of what she was doing, her hand reached out to comfort him. She held his cold fingers. He looked at her with a different kind of longing then. Maybe no one had ever tried to comfort him before. He jerked his hand away as if her pity were too painful for him to endure. But before his hand left hers, a deeper knowledge seeped into her fingers. There was a part of him that wanted to escape his dark destiny.

"Maybe there is a way to reclaim your soul," she offered.

"It was my choice," he insisted.

"You can make another choice."

"You can't understand what it means to have lost hope, because you still have it." He seemed angry now.

"I'm sorry," she said quietly.

She thought he was going to cry, but instead he smiled. That was far worse. It was a sad imitation of a smile, devoid of warmth and joy.

"Party time." His foot slammed on the accelerator and the car skidded around the corner.

The new street was filled with cars and people waiting for the next band to play. Music blasted from car radios and heart-thumping stereos. Richter-scale blasts vibrated the cars' exteriors. Girls sat in car windows, waving and flirting and flaunting their bodies. Guys in low-crotch jeans and baseball hats with clique initials showed off their custom cars. Others cruised looking for girls, checking things out.

Stanton parked the car. He got out, walked around the car, and opened her door. He put his hands around her waist and lifted her out. Only then did she realize how incredibly strong he was.

He kissed her then, a surprise, but so gentle and sweet, she let him. She wondered if Persephone had fallen in love with Hades when he abducted her and took her to live in the underworld. There must be a way to rescue him from this, she thought.

He put his arm around her and shoved through the crowd of kids waiting to go back inside the warehouse.

At the entrance, two large security guards frisked boys and opened purses. They confiscated pencils and pens, anything that could be turned into a weapon.

"Everything out of your pockets," a huge security guard said to Stanton. "Anything I find left in your pockets is mine."

Stanton glared at the man. "I don't think so."

The security guard took a stunned step backward as if he had seen something in Stanton's eyes that made him afraid.

Stanton pushed around him and he and

Vanessa entered the warehouse. It was noisy inside and Vanessa could feel the impatience rising in the crowd, anxious for the music to start again.

Security guards righted white metal barriers and set them in front of the stage. A large sign hung above them: MOSHING AND CROWD SURFING NOT ALLOWED.

Catty stood between Cassandra and Tymmie. She didn't smile when she saw Vanessa. She looked quickly away. But not before Tymmie caught her look and followed it to Vanessa. He nudged Cassandra. The razor cuts on her chest were now covered with scabs. She looked at Vanessa with a hungry smile.

"How do I surrender my power?" Vanessa whispered to Stanton as the band ran onstage. The restless audience screamed and applauded.

"You don't," Stanton said and stepped away.

"I thought we were going to trade."

"Sorry."

"For what?" she asked.

"I lied," he said simply.

The music started with a piercing scream. The crowd crushed forward, knocking over two barriers. Stanton jumped back as the crowd surged toward the stage.

Vanessa was squished into the mob. Then she saw Catty. She struggled around bobbing bodies over to her.

"You shouldn't have come," Catty yelled. "Now they'll have you, too!"

Vanessa looked at the faces of the kids around them. Most of them were ordinary moshers, ravers, and punkers, but then she saw the angry faces of Cassandra, Tymmie, and Karyl staring back at her. Too late, she realized the plan had always been to destroy them both. It was so obvious now. Stanton had betrayed her. But why shouldn't he? What had made her trust him? Maggie had warned her.

Cassandra and Karyl pressed closer. She could feel their thoughts invade her mind, a spectacle of swirling terrifying pictures.

"Don't look in their eyes," Catty warned, and yanked her away.

The band went full speed into punk rock.

The crowd around them exploded into thrashing fists and jumping bodies, knocking Cassandra and Karyl away.

Security guards ran to the slam pit and tried to stop the hitting and shoving and head butting, but it was like trying to stop a train.

Vanessa grabbed Catty's hand as the fury of the crowd shoved them deeper into the mosh pit away from the Followers. A boy tore off his T-shirt and climbed on the shoulders of his friends. Hands grabbed him, held, touched, and pulled him across the heads of the audience, crowd surfing.

A girl climbed onto the stage, struggled around the security guards, and jumped into the crowd. Vanessa ducked as the girl landed on the sea of hands. Catty ducked too late. The girl's boot thumped Catty hard in the forehead.

Surrender, Goddess. The thought hit Vanessa with the sharp strike of a headache. She turned quickly. Cassandra, Karyl, and Tymmie were back. Karyl's eyes caught her and seemed to expand. She had a sudden mental image of Catty crushed beneath jumping feet. Karyl smiled, his eyes deep and mocking. Had he done that? She winced and the trance broke.

The music became a clash of air-ripping tones and head-splintering beats. The thrum of guitars and drums pulsated in Vanessa's head, but it was the other pounding inside her mind that frightened her. Karyl and Tymmie and Cassandra pushed into her thoughts. *Turn. Come back.* She crawled on the sticky floor through jumping, kicking bodies. She was only three feet from Catty now, an impossible distance.

Cassandra's thoughts grabbed Vanessa and twisted into her mind. *You're mine now, Goddess.* Cassandra sent the words screaming through Vanessa's head. She look at Vanessa and smiled, her pale face and garish makeup looked hellish in the flash of the strobe light. Vanessa tried to laugh. What had Maggie said about water on a flame? But she couldn't make her mind focus. She looked in Cassandra's blank eyes and saw tiny images of herself imprisoned in the black pupils. A cold electric feeling invaded her mind like tiny metal worms. Her fears and worries suddenly fell away. Only Cassandra's eyes and Vanessa's need to obey her remained.

Someone bumped into them and the two moon amulets hanging around Vanessa's neck slid against each other. Silver sparks flew from the metals, and Cassandra's eyes flashed with white fire as bright sparks burned into her skin. Vanessa blinked. The spell was broken. Her fear returned. She yanked away, lost her balance, and sprawled on top of Catty. She tried to protect Catty from the hammering feet.

A heavy metal guy in a black T-shirt and silver chains saw their trouble and attempted to help them up, but Karyl appeared from nowhere and head-butted him. The boy staggered back, clutching his forehead.

The music became louder and sent the audience into renewed frenzy. Girls unbuttoned their blouses and flashed the band.

Vanessa reached for Catty's hand. Maybe she could make them both invisible. She tried to concentrate but each kick sent new pain racking through her.

So much for the warrior, she thought and gave in to the hurricane of trampling feet.

Kids surfed the crowd and slammed about.

No one noticed Vanessa and Catty being tram-
pled on the mosh pit floor.

Vanessa felt herself melting into the pain
that tore through her body when a hand grabbed
her and pulled her up.

CHAPTER TWENTY-FIVE

KARYL DRAGGED VANESSA away from the crowd.

"Failed goddess," he smirked. "Look in my eyes to save your friend."

She knew it was another lie, but she was too weak to pull away. His eyes held hers. She felt herself falling again. Another memory? It was different this time. She could feel hope ebbing from her. Was this what Morgan felt? An inhospitable cold swirled deep inside her and still she could not look away.

"Stop," she begged. She doubted Karyl could

hear her over the maelstrom of music. She continued to fall. Her lungs burned for oxygen. Her heart was on fire. She felt dizzy. The dizziness brought up tears and unhappy dreams from some hidden place behind her heart where she had tucked so many disappointments. Tears pushed into her eyes.

Then she heard someone calling, the voice barely audible, like a whisper on the wind. Impossible. It had to be her imagination. A voice in her mind was telling her not to look. It was Stanton.

If you look too long in his eyes, Stanton's voice whispered across her mind, *you'll be lost. He's stealing your life force, your hope.*

She closed her eyes.

"Look at me," Karyl ordered, shaking her.

She felt Karyl push away, and then Stanton took her in his arms.

"Come to my world," Stanton ordered. "It's the only way I can save you."

"Save me?"

"They will destroy you."

"But I'm the key. Don't they need me?"

"No, Vanessa, you're not the key," Stanton said. "It's a special night for the Atrox. If two Daughters of the Moon are destroyed during the night of the Nefandus moon, the power balance shifts in favor of the dark. The only way I can save you now is to make you one of us. Of your own free will, join me to save yourself."

At that moment, she wanted him and his world. Why not give up the struggle? It would be so easy. She shook her head. "What about the people I'm supposed to protect?"

"Save yourself," he repeated.

"I don't want a life like yours."

"I can't harm you, because you performed an act of kindness to save me when I was a boy," he said. "But I can't protect you from the others."

Karyl ripped her away from Stanton and he let her go without a struggle. She could feel Karyl in her mind like an electrical current and already part of her wanted to turn and gaze in his eyes and fall into that sweet dangerous peace.

With renewed energy and determination she fought the images Karyl was pushing into her mind and pictured the full moon instead. She wasn't going to die like this. Power filled her body. She closed her eyes and let her mind expand to the ends of the universe. Her molecules loosened. She floated through his grasping hands.

She found Catty and became visible again. She didn't care who might see. She tore Catty's amulet from her own neck and pressed it into Catty's hand. It had been a long time since she had tried to make anyone invisible with her, and her powers were weak.

She held Catty's hand as the Followers pushed through the crowd toward them. She could feel Cassandra's thoughts clasp hold. And then Tymmie's. She was determined not to let them overpower her this time. Her amulet began to glow. Energy seared through her like a burst of flame. She pulled Catty up and stood as Karyl attacked.

"Vanessa," Catty warned weakly.

A strange light from the amulet struck Karyl's face and he instantly stepped back, surprised. What had stopped him? The amulet? Did it have powers?

Cassandra and Tymmie circled, a strange grin of torment on their faces.

"Why aren't they attacking?" Catty said.

Vanessa didn't answer. She couldn't. The power inside her felt too strong. It pulsed through every cell. Then an unearthly glow shimmered protectively around them and they rose like silver smoke into the air.

They floated over the crowd. As they neared the exit, something drew her eyes back to Stanton. He was charming and handsome in a threatening and seductive way. He stared up at her even though she was sure he couldn't see her. He had betrayed her, then saved her, only to betray her again. But looking at him now and seeing how sad he looked, she felt sorry for him. She thought of his offer. Did he love her? Too late she realized she shouldn't have looked back. She had lost her concentration. Her molecules clustered.

Catty became dense and slipped from her grasp. Her molecules reformed rapidly and she dropped toward the crowd. Vanessa tumbled close behind her.

They hit the crowd. Hands grabbed their arms, legs, and stomachs and carried them over the bobbing heads.

Vanessa prayed the swell of hands would carry them to the barricades and drop them into the arms of the waiting security guards. Then they could run backstage and out to safety.

But the hands carried them the wrong way, back to the Followers.

CHAPTER TWENTY-SIX

THE HANDS DROPPED Vanessa in front of Cassandra.

"Goddess." Cassandra said the word like a curse.

"Nice to have you back." Tymmie grinned, his eyes blank and deep.

They crowded around her, their thoughts pushing into her mind. She tried to escape through the mangle of pounding arms and feet, but when she saw Karyl clutching Catty, something sparked inside her. She flung herself at him. He stumbled backward, stunned. Too late she remembered Maggie's warning about using the tools of the Atrox. He turned and snickered. His thin face fired with a horrible rage, and his pupils dilated.

Vanessa steadied herself for his assault, but it never came. She opened her eyes.

Karyl stood still, staring at the entrance. The throng in the mosh pit stopped jumping and pushing. Faces turned. The singer in the band lost his words and stared at something in the audience.

The crowd stood still. Something bigger than the full-speed rock hysteria had taken hold.

"What's going on?" Catty asked.

"I don't know yet." And then Vanessa knew. "It's Serena and Jimena."

Serena and Jimena walked into the crowd, strides long and seductive. Jimena wore a silver bustier and capris with matching sandals. Her hair was rolled on top of her head with glitter and jewels. Curls bounced with each step. Her face gleamed; her full lips sparkled. The tattoos on her arms seemed iridescent. She whooped and squealed and gave Serena a high five.

Serena had moussed her hair so it stood on

end. Streaks of orange glitter shot from her temples into her hair. She wore a yellow tulle skirt over a sheer, clingy red dress and looked like a walking flame.

The strobe light flickered, making the entire room surreal.

"Non aliquis incipit convivium sine nobis," Jimena yelled.

"Nos sumus convivium!" Serena joined in.

Vanessa wondered if it was a curse or an incantation.

Their silver moon amulets caught the flashing strobe light and threw magic rainbows across the faces of the Followers. Cassandra squealed and put her hands in front of her eyes. Tymmie and Karyl glared.

"Hey, boys," Jimena said to the band and stood with her hand on a hip thrust to the side. "Where's the music? We came here to party."

The bass player smiled. The drummer nodded, and music crashed through the room. The velocity gained with each beat of the drum. The guitars sent metallic notes into the air like machine-gun fire. The corrugated walls of the warehouse vibrated. The mosh pit spun into slam dancing.

Vanessa felt a strange thrum against her chest. She looked down. The light from her own amulet was so strong she had to look away.

Serena gestured to Karyl and Tymmie, wiggling her fingers in an enticing way "Come on, bad boys, we're here to play. That's what you wanted."

Tymmie and Karyl smiled dangerously. Their power came like an invisible wave pushing against her. Vanessa took an involuntary step backward. The force of their thoughts didn't seem to affect Jimena or Serena.

"Well?" Jimena was expectant, head cocked to one side.

Cassandra joined Tymmie and Karyl. Her thoughts came like hellish screams. Vanessa grabbed her ears, even though she knew the piercing noise was inside her head.

Jimena and Serena stood perfectly still, as if the screams didn't bother them.

Frustrated, Cassandra lunged and swung. Jimena ducked. The nails missed Jimena's cheek by inches. Jimena shined the light from her amulet into Cassandra's eyes.

Cassandra grabbed her eyes and tumbled away. But it was something more than the amulet that had stopped Cassandra. Vanessa could feel it now, a dangerously benevolent power that billowed from Jimena and Serena.

Tymmie grabbed Serena and Karyl stared into her eyes. The pupils in Serena's eyes expanded. Vanessa could feel the force of their struggle. Her head pounded with the energy.

Finally, Karl stumbled backward. Then Serena swung around and shined her amulet in Tymmie's eyes, but again Vanessa knew it was something more than the power of the amulet that made Tymmie look confused and stagger before he turned and ran.

Serena turned to face Karyl again. The skin tightened against his skull as if anger and hatred burned inside him. His power vibrated through Vanessa in an ominously exciting way, his thoughts sweetly seductive and irresistible. Her eyes drifted to him. She wondered if Serena was also drowning in his eyes.

Then Jimena touched her. She snapped back with a wrench of her neck.

"Take Catty and go outside to the car." She stood protectively in front of them.

Vanessa concentrated until she and Catty were as weightless as moonbeams. Then they drifted up and over the crowd. She glanced down at Stanton. She could feel his eyes saying their battle wasn't done. She looked away.

Outside fog had settled on the ground. She pulled her molecules together and slowly drifted back to earth next to Jimena's car.

Catty hugged her fiercely. She almost lost her balance. "Thank you, Vanessa."

"How did they catch you?" Vanessa squeezed Catty tightly.

"I was doing my leapfrog back to Saturday night. It worked," she said with excitement. "But Karyl, Tymmie, and Cassandra were following you that night at the Bowl. I got too close, and they grabbed me. I was so drained from all the time-twisting that I couldn't get away. They kept me prisoner. You can't imagine what it was like reliving time with them. I still can't figure out why they were following you. "

"There's something I've been wanting to tell you," Vanessa began. "You're not a space alien."

"No?" Catty's voice seemed disappointed. "What am I, then?"

"A goddess."

"Yeah, right, would a goddess have trouble pulling a comb through her hair? Or get so many bruises?" She held out her arms.

"For real, not a space person, you're a goddess."

"A goddess," Catty repeated, as if she were tasting the word. "Yeah, I always knew."

"You did not." Vanessa laughed.

"Sure I did," Catty said, and then she was crying in Vanessa's arms.

Serena and Jimena ran out to the car, exhilarated and glowing.

"¡Ándale! Hurry," Jimena urged, "before they get to changing their minds and decide they want to fight some more."

They climbed in the car. Jimena turned the key in the ignition. The mufflers thundered.

As the car pulled away, a new worry filled Vanessa. She had promised Maggie she wouldn't meet Stanton, and now she had defied her. She was sure there was going to be a punishment. Would she take away her power? She didn't want to lose it now. Her stomach churned with apprehension.

Jimena stopped the car in front of Maggie's apartment and got out. She turned to Vanessa. "Maggie said we had to bring you back here after.

They walked up to the front door and pushed the security button. There was no answer.

"Push it again," Serena said.

Suddenly Maggie appeared, breathless, behind them. "Sorry I'm late. I had to take Vanessa's friend Morgan home."

"She's all right?" Vanessa asked.

"Of course."

Then Vanessa took a deep breath. She didn't know if she should try to apologize now, or wait until after Maggie told her what her punishment would be.

"Vanessa . . ." Maggie started.

"I know I failed," Vanessa cut in, and felt hot tears press into her eyes.

"Failed? No, not at all."

"I didn't fail? But you made me promise to do nothing. You said I had no choice."

"I had to test you, Vanessa," Maggie said. "Yes, I needed to make sure you were willing to risk everything to do what was right. Saving Catty was the right choice." She placed her soft hand on Vanessa's cheek. "You are one of those daughters upon whom Selene has bestowed great gifts. She has given you magnanimity of spirit, physical energy, and courage."

Vanessa felt a strange glow tremble through her. She glanced at Serena and Jimena and saw relief on their faces as well, and then she looked at Catty, who looked totally confused.

"Welcome, my last daughter."

Catty smiled. "You're the lady from my dreams. You're real! How cool!"

They went upstairs to the apartment. The room smelled of ginger and cinnamon and glowed from candles placed around the room. The table was set for tea. They sat down and Maggie poured tea as Serena and Jimena told her what had happened.

"You all did well tonight," Maggie praised

them. "And to think this is the Nefandus Moon, a dark moon special to the Atrox. Very good, my dears."

"They're not defeated," Jimena said.

"But they're been stopped on a very momentous night, and my daughters are still together."

Maggie talked quickly as she wrapped Catty's arms in bandages and applied a slippery goo to the cut on her forehead. She told Catty everything that she had explained to Vanessa about the Atrox and its followers. When she finished, she added something Vanessa hadn't heard before: "Your gift only lasts until you are seventeen, and then there's a metamorphosis. You have to make the most important choice of your life. Either you can choose to lose your powers and your memory of what you once were, or you disappear. The ones who disappear become something else, guardian spirits perhaps. No one really knows."

The girls sat silently, taking it all in.

Then Vanessa remembered the strange words that Serena and Jimena had spoken. "What were the incantations you yelled when you came in to rescue Catty and me?"

"Non aliquis incipit convivium sine nobis," Jimena said.

"Nos sumus convivium," Serena finished.

Maggie looked at them sternly. "That's what you said?"

Jimena nodded. "It means 'No one starts the party without us.'"

"Yeah, 'cause we are the party!" Serena grinned and then they were all laughing.

"But wait." Catty put her hand up and touched the poultice that Maggie had put over the bruise on her forehead. "How did you know where to find us?"

"That's easy." Serena looked at Jimena. "She had a premonition."

"Yeah, I saw you all dolled up in blue." Jimena smiled at Vanessa.

"But I didn't even know where I was going." Vanessa leaned back in her chair, bewildered.

"It's not like reading minds," Serena explained.

"I saw the warehouse." Jimena tapped the side of her head with her finger. "I used to be one of the girls who hung out there, so I knew where to go."

"So how did you fight them?" Vanessa asked.

"The amulets." Serena cupped her hand around hers. "They give us power."

"Now, I've told you that's not it," Maggie warned. "The amulets are only symbols. They mean nothing without your faith. It is your faith in yourselves to turn their evil away that makes you stronger than they are."

"But the amulets glowed," Catty pointed out.

"That was your power, my dear." Maggie spoke softly. "The amulet is only a reminder of the power inside you. Each of you has a special power to fight the Atrox. Jimena's premonitions will tell us when someone needs our help. Serena with her mind-reading will know when someone is being tempted by the Atrox. Vanessa's invisibility will enable her to go among the Followers unseen and tell us what they are planning. And Catty can travel into the past or future to confirm our suspicions so that the Followers cannot deceive us. Together you are an unstoppable force."

The girls looked at each other and smiled.

"Why does the dark of the moon give me the creeps?" Vanessa sipped the tea.

"Evil forces are stronger in darkness. I suppose some would blame Selene for the dark moon." Maggie turned her face away. "There wasn't always a dark of the moon, you know."

"What happened?" Catty asked.

"Selene was responsible for guiding the moon across the skies. One night Selene looked down and saw Endymion in the hills, the most beautiful man, a shepherd."

Vanessa thought of Michael. Then she blushed and looked around the table.

Maggie cleared her throat. "She fell in love. First sight. All that heart-flipping, adrenaline-surging wonder of it. She couldn't resist him. She crept down to lie beside him, abandoning her duty. Some say she asked Zeus to make Endymion sleep for eternity so she would always have him with her. But the truth is Zeus was so angered by the darkened sky that he punished Selene and made it so Endymion should sleep forever. But that didn't stop Selene from loving him. She slips away for a few nights each month to visit her sleeping lover and see if she can wake him."

"What would happen if she did wake him?" Jimena asked.

"After all these years I 'd hate to consider the consequences. She'd probably stay away for months, wreak havoc with the tides and weather." Maggie started laughing. "What would scientists think of their theories then? Gravity?" she said as if it were an absurd idea and laughed some more.

At sunrise, Catty and Vanessa walked home.

"Wow, what an adventure," Catty said. "Let's go back and do it again."

"No!" Vanessa grabbed Catty's arm. She looked at her watch. The hands were gratefully still.

"Just kidding." Catty laughed and hugged her.

CHAPTER TWENTY-SEVEN

WHEN VANESSA CREPT back in her bedroom, she found a red velvet pillow leaning against her other pillows on her bed. She picked it up. GODDESS was embroidered in deeper reds and golds on the front.

"Stanton," she whispered and stared at the pillow. She was going to toss it, but something made her hold it tight.

"Goddess," she read again, and smiled.

She took a long shower, letting the hot water wash the glitter and paint from her body. She crawled into bed and didn't bother to close the window. She sensed that she was safe, for now. She curled against the red velvet pillow and fell asleep thinking about Michael.

She woke later that day, a little stunned by all that had happened, and dressed. Catty had planned to spend the day in bed sleeping, but Vanessa had two things to do that couldn't wait.

At dusk, she walked down Fairfax Avenue carrying the lawn flamingo she had purchased at Armstrong's. She turned down Melrose Avenue and walked for several blocks, past boutiques named Street Slut and Wizard, then turned again. She found the house with the missing flamingo and set the new one in the ground.

She still had something important to do. It was risky, but she felt she owed it to herself. She walked over to Michael's house and knocked on the door.

"Vanessa," Michael said in surprise when he opened the door.

She pretended not to see his look of irritation. "I just wanted you to know that none of the things I did were ever about you."

He looked confused.

"I had something going on in my life. Something that made me act odd at times, but it's nothing to do with you. I really like you. And I wanted to kiss you and I wanted to hold your hand, but when you touch me, I get nervous and I feel all crazy inside and I act weird." She stopped. Was he smiling?

She started again. "And I'm probably never going to stop acting the way I do, because that's just who I am."

She looked back at him. Why didn't he say anything?

"Well, there, I said it. That's the truth."

He still didn't say anything.

"So I wanted to let you know that."

She bit her lip, shrugged, then turned and walked away feeling totally humiliated.

"Vanessa," Michael called.

Her heart flipped. She turned back. He was definitely smiling.

"You want to go to Planet Bang with me Tuesday night?"

"Yes." Did she answer too quickly? Her

molecules buzzed in a dreamy way, and she smiled back at him. "Yeah, I'd like that."

"I'll pick you up early, and we'll eat first."

She nodded. "That sounds great."

"You want to come in? I was just playing the piano."

She smiled mischievously and walked toward him. "No," she whispered and looked deep into his eyes.

"No?" he teased.

And then he reached out, and his arms were around her. She breathed in the spice soap smell of him. He bent his head down, and his lips pressed against hers. Waves of desire rose inside her. Her molecules swirled in pleasure, but they stayed together tight and strong. She let him kiss her again before she stopped him. Then she opened her eyes and looked at him.

"So I'll see you at school tomorrow," she said, and turned to leave.

"Tomorrow." He grinned.

"Bye." She blew him a kiss and hurried down the walk.

And then she was running back to Melrose.

She looked up and saw the crescent moon. She glanced behind her. The street was empty. She smiled and let her molecules go. Her spirits soared. She sailed beyond the neighborhood toward Hollywood. Catty was right. It was a gift. She wished she had used it more.

Soon she flowed above a boy selling souvenir maps to the stars' homes for eight dollars. The maps were years old. Most of the stars no longer lived at the addresses listed on the cover.

She concentrated. "Three maps, please," she said in a ghostly whisper.

The boy looked up and down, then turned completely around.

She laughed, a phantom in the wind, and caught the next breeze.

At Hollywood and Vine, a bus filled with camera-clicking tourists drove by. On a whim she funneled through an open bus window. Then, in her best Marilyn Monroe voice, she whispered, "Welcome to Hollywood, my fine folks."

The tourists looked bewildered, astonished.

"Don't be afraid," she said. "I'm just Tinsel Town magic."

The tourists clapped.

She spent twenty minutes being Marilyn's ghost and making tourists laugh. Then she spilled out the window to a burst of applause and waited for the next breeze.

The wind picked up and carried her away. She could stay invisible forever. She didn't completely understand her power, but she was beginning to understand who she was. *Goddess*, she thought, and her molecules formed a smile before she rode the breeze with arc-shaped leaps, like a dolphin, up and down toward home.

r

Don't miss the next

DAUGHTERS OF THE MOON book,

into the cold fire.

"WHAT'S UP?" Jimena asked Serena.

"Can we just go now?"

"Sure." Jimena didn't hesitate. They started walking toward the door.

Outside, Serena tried to push into Jimena's mind but it was like a stone wall. "What is it you don't want me to see?" she said in an accusing tone.

"What do you mean?"

"You know what I mean."

Jimena was silent. Her lips tightened.

"I thought you said we were always going to keep it real," Serena pleaded. "Always real between you and me."

"I had a premonition," Jimena began slowly.

Serena waited. Her heart beat rapidly.

"I saw you standing in the cold fire," Jimena whispered. "That's what we've all been hiding from you. We didn't want you to worry."

"You think I'm going to become a Follower?" Fear trembled through Serena's body. "How could you not have told me?"

"We're watching over you," Jimena assured her. "We'll make sure it doesn't come true."

"But you've never been able to stop any of your premonitions from coming true."

Jimena was silent for a long time and when she finally spoke, her voice broke. "I know," she said sadly.

DAUGHTERS OF THE MOON

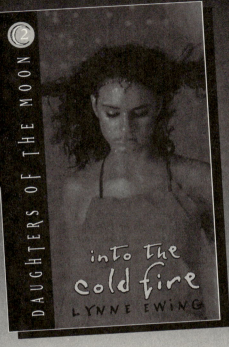

Jimena has premonitions and she has never been wrong before. . . . When she has a vision of Serena betraying the Daughters of the Moon, can the girls band together to stop her?

Find out in

DAUGHTERS OF THE MOON #2
into the cold fire